CURIOSITIES

NUMBER TWO

SPRING
2018

CME

Curiosities #2 Spring 2018.
©2018 by Kevin Frost

"Dem Bones"©2017 by Ann Stolinsky.
"East Wind in Carrall Street"©2016 by Holly Schofield, first appeared in *Clockwork Canada* and *ELQ/Exile: The Literary Quarterly,* Exile Editions.
"On The Path"©2009 by Kelly A. Harmon, first published in *Triangulation: Dark Glass,* Parsec Ink Publishing.
"Only Gutter Girls And Ruined Things" ©2017 by Julia K. Patt.
"Pet Shop"©2016 by Gary Buller.
"Seeded"©2017 by Susan Taitel.
"The Analytical Engine of Hester Watts, Grand Mistress of the Unseen"©2018 by Laura Duerr.
"The Ghost-Extinguisher" by Gelett Burgess, illustrated by George T. Tobin, first published in *The Cosmopolitan,* April 1905, and is in the public domain (USA, works before 1923).
"The Stolen Child"©2017 by Gavin Bradley.
"The Thousand Injuries"©2017 by Eric Cline.

Cover art: "Gate" ©2017 by Justin Tiang.
Clip art sourced from The British Library's Flickr albums.

ISBN-13: 978-1-948396-01-1 (print)

TABLE OF CONTENTS

I have often thought that I should have been born a Finn, as I have never been much for wordiness. But if I do not write now, then this issue will never make it to press in a timely manner. So.

As I was cleaning out my old laptop which was showing signs of imminent failure, I came upon a hefty folder labeled "possible stories." It was stuffed full of old horror stories I had downloaded from free story websites, and, sorted by topic. Most would be painful reminders of why I decided to start buying new fiction in order to continue my podcast project, rather than continue the time consuming and increasingly unproductive mining of available online public domain archives.

The problem with public domain works is that they are too often too... *something.* Too long. Too rambling. Too dull. Too done. Too racist. And, if not outright misogynistic, mostly lacking in female characters who did more than act as furniture or convenient murder victims. But there were some good stories in there that I never got around to recording and were still worth reading. I decided to select those that were not well known (those of a certain age may recall how there were stories which always seemed to appear in every other anthology you picked up at the library when you were first reading in the adult section), held up to a modern reading, and especially those that had some sort of cultural relevance in our era.

Which brought up the question of abridgement.

Should we?

I was torn. Stories from before about 1850 are quaintly nested, Canterbury Tales style, to be told in the context of groups of travelers sitting around a fire in a public house, especially if there is an element of the fantastic. It wasn't too much trouble to surgically extract those, and I do think we should not paint a rosy picture of the past, and should read old works keeping in mind the context of when they were written. But if one is to read primarily for entertainment, the appearance of certain words can be a stumbling block that can detract from the intent of the story.

For this issue, I chose "The Ghost-Extinguisher" by Gelett Burgess, which can be found in the April 1905 issue of *The Cosmopolitan,* tucked between articles on German Army man-euvers and the proper use of crop rotation. The story is not widely known, but it does have significance to popular culture, as I think you will discover. I had not read it in a while, but I remembered it as a humorous piece. There couldn't possibly be anything in this one that was going to trip me up.

Wrong.

Right there in the first act was a word that this white kid from San Francisco would never use except to describe a particular type of footwear that was popular in the 1970s. And even that was said with a hint of embarrassment. What was the right approach to take? I swallowed my social anxiety and introduced myself to experienced editors and writers at a nearby science fiction convention to ask them if there was an established approach to editing public domain works. It did not appear to be a comfortable subject for anyone.

In the end, I made the decision to abridge, and for the sake of transparency, it is right that I say so in the introductory pages and give you my reasoning. I think I have made it as seamless as possible. The original unabridged version can easily be found online through any search engine. I also think you will recognize this story, even if you have not encountered it before. It made me smile when I first discovered it. And I love seeing glimpses of what

San Francisco was like before the earthquake.

We are new editors, and the learning curve is steep. Our current plan is to publish thrice yearly, and continue to produce a podcast twice a month. Text editing is not nearly as time consuming as processing audio for podcast, and I've found that I enjoy the process. It is time to accept that not every story we buy is going to make it to broadcast, despite our best efforts, but now they will all be published and read. We did not purchase print or electronic rights on the stories we bought in our first year, so it is unlikely that the stories on the earlier shows will ever appear here.

Finally, thanks to the reading and editing crew Andrew McCurdy and Jed Dagger, and Steadman Kondor who joined us this year. And dear Uncle Osgoode who keeps us from taking things too seriously.

Kevin Frost
New Mexico
March 2018

On the Path
Kelly A. Harmon

The soul-powered plow halted mid-furrow and hastened to a shuddering stop as the reincarnation engine seized up.

"Not again," said Tân, swinging his legs to the side of the wooden tank and jumping down out of the seat. As he stepped forward to check the soul-seal, the cap fired off with a hollow thud, like a cork from a jug.

Thick white steam, more creamy than translucent, escaped the ruptured tank with a shrill whistle, erupting geyser-straight into the air until a strong gust of north wind blew it toward Zhourong. Tân could almost hear the screams of the souls in the din.

"*Ma-de!*" he yelled, pulling off his gloves and slapping them on the tank. "Curse you to hell if you touch my wife or children!" he shouted to the escaping vapor. "Leave them alone or I'll kill you the moment you're reborn."

Thank the gods the steaming cloud moved toward town and away from his home. The south wind had blown the last time this happened. He remembered that time well: both his wife and two teenage daughters became pregnant that night. His youngest child was eight, his two grandchildren the same age, all born only days apart.

That accident brought both joy and pain. Three more mouths to feed indebted him to the temple, for he could not pay his promised offerings on time. Yet he'd been blessed with more children, and grandchildren, who would grow up together. And he'd been compensated with larger herds. He'd earned two additional milk cows, several twins of sheep—doubling the flock—and the chickens destined for the soup pot all laid eggs the very same night. He'd siphoned the souls off those eggs after cracking them for breakfast the next morning.

But those souls had been infantile and had powered his reincarnation engine for less than a year.

These souls he'd worked more than eight years—they were not young like the others. They'd spent time in the engines for which they should be compensated on their journey to Tao. What happened to escaped souls after spending eight years on the path of reincarnation? He was certain he didn't want to know.

Tàn looked back at the ruptured tank. It's silk-smooth sides and dark, oiled wood denoted many years of loving use and care. Could he forget about it? Ignore the tank breach and continue as if nothing had happened? He'd have to revert back to manual farming—and Heng and his daughters would have to join him in the fields. He shook his head. I don't want it to come to that, he thought. Yet, he didn't know if he could do this a second time.

The north wind blew again, cutting through the high collar of his quilted tunic and Tàn shivered. He plucked his bamboo hat off and ran a calloused hand through greying black strands escaped from his waist-length queue and walked to the mud-brick cabin he shared with his wife, daughters and grandchildren.

Yes, he could do this again: admit the failure of the tank to the priests, start once more with a new batch of souls—It was easier than asking his family to help.

Mud sucked at his clogs as Tân neared his home. He'd reserved the driest section of land for the grain fields, and as a result, the house wallowed in mud in the rainy season. To compensate, Tân had raised the building up and built a wrapping porch around all four sides of it. In the summer, he and his family slept outside upon the wide deck, in much more spacious comfort than their tiny rooms allowed.

He walked up the four steps to the porch, kicked off his shoes, and stepped over the raised sill of the door before entering the house.

"Heng?" he called, pushing in the wooden door.

She looked up from the steaming pot of rice on the brick stove.

"Ai?" She smiled, settling the lid back on the pot and walking toward Tân. She halted at his next words.

"We have need of a priest," he said. "The tank on the reincarnation engine burst again."

Heng moved her hands to her womb, pressing against it, as if to block entry.

"The wind is blowing north," he said. "You have nothing to worry about."

Slowly, Heng lowered her hands, as if not quite believing. She looked to the tiny, crowded altar in a small alcove in the rear of the house. "Shall we...?"

"Yes, of course," he said. "There's no sense jinxing our luck."

He walked to the altar and bowed, then lifted three new sticks of incense, lit them from a ceremonial candle and placed them in a burner.

Without being asked, Heng gathered together a sack of tangerines for Tân to take as an offering to the temple.

Tân climbed the mountain to the temple.

Compared to the Bogda Feng, this mountain was a hillock, but knowing that didn't make the climb any easier. *Old Grandfather,* he prayed to the father of all gods, *I understand the need for the privacy of those who serve the Gods, but could not this privacy be found on less steep ground?*

Then he saw the red-headed crane, a sign of luck, and immortality. He bowed to the crane, and continued. Perhaps Old Grandfather sent him a sign by way of the bird.

The temple abutted the mountain face on a narrow plateau near a narrow, rapid stream. A slender footbridge, painted red with yellow lotus blossoms and hung with tiny brass bells arched over the small stream and deposited those who crossed to within a few feet of the temple.

Tân could see that the rice-paper door of the temple stood wide. Three priests sat cross-legged on the porch in a bit of watery sunshine. Eyes closed, they breathed as one, hands in their laps, clasped in *Zhen's Supplication.* Inside the temple, a free-standing altar squatted behind them, wisps of burning incense whorling to the ceiling.

The smell of honeysuckle, his favorite blossom, reached Tân before he set foot on the bridge. Smiling, he decided the monk's choice of incense must be, like the crane, another sign of good luck.

Tân walked across the bridge, bells jangling with each step, discordant in the quiet of the mountainside. Below, the current sang over the rocks, peaceful in comparison to the clangor of the bells.

He stopped on the other side and bowed, waiting for the priests to acknowledge him.

"Only those seeking favors climb the mountain bearing gifts," said first-priest Sheng. She lifted a mask at her side, and donned the face of the Jade Emperor who sits in judgment in heaven: his eyes and ears larger than life in order to see and hear all he needs to know.

Tân bowed, shucked his clogs and stepped onto the porch. "My soul tank has ruptured again. I need to purchase additional souls."

"You have awful luck with reincarnation engines," Sheng said, "Perhaps you should consider a more traditional mode of farming."

She lowered the mask.

"I have considered it," said Tân, "but—."

"But what about your donations to the temple?" she asked. Beside her, Li and Hu nodded their heads.

Hu said, "Your crops would be smaller, and you might still give thirty percent to the temple. But thirty percent of a reduced donation will slow your path to salvation..." He drew a line in the sandy floor with a black, lacquered nail filed to a precise point, "the paths of your wife and children, too."

Li stood, donning the mask of Guan Yin and taking the position of *Guan's Hauteur:* one hand on her chin, the other clasping the upraised elbow. "You have grandchildren, too, do you not, Tân?" she asked. "Have your daughters married yet?"

She relaxed the position and tugged a carved, jade barrette from her topknot, letting loose a cascade of hair that nearly touched the saffron-yellow embroidery on the hem of her purple robes.

Tân felt anger growing in his chest. This was not the conversation he'd come to have. He'd come to buy souls and get back to the fields. He hadn't time to discuss the philosophy of Tao.

They knew he'd chosen to farm wheat and barley because it was harder than flooding his fields and wallowing in rice like every other farmer. His uncommon crops yielded enough money to buy his way past the lower stages of salvation. And if Old Grandfather willed it, the paths of his entire family. His methods were not just self-serving, he hoped to smooth the way for them all. Is that not what a father does for his children?

He closed his eyes.

Grandfather, he prayed, *please see me through this trial with money enough to skip ahead on the path to Tao. And please grant me the ability to remain calm in your temple, among your most ardent followers.*

He opened his eyes.

Grandfather willing, he and his family would spend no time in the soul tanks. Years in a reincarnation engine only to be expelled in a single steaming overload into the belly of a nearby cow, or gods forbid, the belly of a chicken—only to be plucked, boiled, eaten and tossed back on a lower path to begin again—that wasn't for him! He could afford to be above that. He'd worked hard and given much.

Wasn't he willing to sacrifice luxuries he could well afford to secure a place in the Tao that much sooner?

He thought, I have scrimped like a millet farmer, worn patched pants, fed my family the meals of a less prosperous man, so to make the path to heaven shorter for my family. Surely, with his work and his money, they could make themselves a place on a higher plane when they died in this lifetime.

Calmness, Grandfather, he thought again.

He turned to Li. "Of course my daughters have not married, honorable one," he said. "Who would have them now?" He bowed over his hat, clasped between his hands.

"You regret their burden?" asked Hu.

"I want them happy," Tân said.

"And out of your house," Sheng said.

Tân stepped back, stricken, almost out of the small temple. His anger fled.

"It's not like that, honorable one," he said. "I would welcome a son-in-law in my home."

"Unusual," said Hu.

"But not unheard of," said Tân. "My home is large enough. The land can support more."

"And sons-in-law could work the land, bring in more income —allowing you to bypass many more stages of reincar-nation on the way to Tao," Sheng said.

"It's allowed," said Tân. A crackle rose up from the brim of his hat, now crushed in his hands.

"But only if you realize what you're giving up," said Sheng.

"I do, honorable one," Tân said, bowing, "hard work, discomfort, prolonged journey."

"This you know," said Hu, "but what about self-sacrifice? You need only be *willing* to skip ahead on the Tao." He stood and turned to the rear wall and plucked a pin from a square of *xuanzhi* paper and lifted it from its place among several others. Tân recognized his name inked on the rice-paper square.

Hu lowered the square along the Tao path and pushed the pin back into the wall.

Tân felt his eyes burn with embarrassment. He stared at the hundreds of squares on the wall, names of his family, his neighbors. He listened to the river play on the rocks beneath the floor of the temple but refused to be soothed. Tân longed to tear his name from the wall, all the names, and dump them in the river as it rushed away down the hill. Biting back the angry words inside him, he bowed and said, "Honorable sir, I do not understand."

"You have not learned from your experience," Hu said.

"But I have paid," Tân said. "My daughters have paid."

"Indeed," Hu said, lifting the rice-paper squares with his daughters' names painted on them, and replacing them fractionally higher than Tân's. "We're certain that your daughters have learned from their experience," Hu said.

He could not be calm. Before he embarrassed himself, Tân bowed—a chicken-like bob of his head, once to each priest, and turned to leave.

"Wait," Sheng said. "Did you not come for more souls?"

Tân wished to deny it and storm from the temple, but without the souls he could not plow as much land. Without the land he could not buy his way to the next plateau on the path.

"Young souls," he demanded, knowing their eagerness to work would provide his plow with more power.

Hu held out a clay jar stoppered on both the top and the bottom with cork, and named a sum three times what Tân had paid the last time.

"Robbery," Tân said. "I won't pay that."

"Is any price too expensive to buy yourself a higher plane of existence?" asked Sheng.

Tàn bowed. "I'd planned to donate two-thirds of what you ask for myself and my family's existential journey."

"Good deeds are worth more," Li said, raising the face of Chun Kwan to mask her own.

"And take much longer, honorable one," Tàn said. He did not remind Li that Chun Kwan did not perform his good deeds until *after* he ascended into the heavens. Instead, Tàn drew a wallet from the bag tied at his waist and handed over payment for the jar.

"We will gladly give over these souls for nothing," said Li, now wearing the smiling mask of the trickster Wu Zhen.

"If?" he asked.

"If you search your heart," said first-priest Sheng, slipping on the well-worn mask of Old Grandfather, "you'll know the answer and will place yourself firmly on the path."

Tàn bowed and walked down the steps, then turned his back to the priests, retrieved his clogs, and made his way homeward, the sound of the wooden soles of his shoes striking off rocks and echoing on the stony path all the way down the hill.

Tàn returned to his fields, stopping first at the small barn for a clay pot of resin from the mawei tree, and walked to the soul engine. He placed the jar of souls bottom-side-down over the mouth of the soul tank, and pulled the cork from the top of the jar.

There was little chance the souls would escape, as cold and thick as they were, but the double-cork mechanism helped to prevent their loss nonetheless. A string connecting the top cork to the bottom assured that both were plucked from the jar simultaneously. After Tan breached the jar, the enclosed souls flowed at a sluggish pace into the tank, plopping softly onto the bottom. Quickly, Tàn removed the jar and capped the tank, sealing it with resin, before the souls realized freedom awaited but a handsbreadth above them.

He turned the crank to stir the souls and lit the pilot light to generate the small bit of heat which was the catalyst to get the souls moving. The engine chugged to life and Tân said the prayer to the gods asking that these souls earn their higher rank on their path to Tao when they were done with their job for him.

He patted the top of the machine like one would pat a workhorse, then loosed the brake and guided it up a furrow.

It may have been a trick of the light, but when he reached the end of the field and turned the plow to the next row, he thought he saw a figure dart among his tangerine trees. Tân tied off the brake, but left the engine running as he made his way into the grove.

Quiet usually reigned in the grove, the dense foliage of the evergreens insulating it from sounds outside. Tân's feet rustled the dried leaves beneath the trees, sounding over loud in his ears, but the noise did not mask the sound of the six figures climbing among his largest tangerine trees.

Two climbed in the top-most boughs, pulling out the ripest, juiciest fruits and tossed them down to the four on the ground. The others sat in the leaves, backs to Tân, pulling the loose skins from the orange-red fruit and devouring them, hands shoving the pulpy fruit into mouths and reaching for another before the first could even be swallowed.

"You there!" he yelled. "Thieves! Get out of my trees."

The rustling stopped, and the two men in the trees jumped to the ground. Those seated, rose and turned to Tân. In the shade of the trees, Tân found it hard to distinguish the features of the thieves, and he took a step forward to confront them, then halted abruptly. He recognized his uncle among them, his father's brother, one of the tree climbers.

His heart thumped in his chest, and he could feel a fine sheen of sweat break out on his forehead. Uncle Lao Weng had died more than twenty years ago. Tân and Heng had been newly wed when he had fallen down the well and drowned.

Tân found his anger leave abruptly. His body shook. He thought he would have been less fearful when meeting the ghost of his own ancestor. Still, he bowed deeply. "Uncle, my apologies. You are, of course, welcome to my tangerines, as are your companions. Is there else you would like?"

He looked closely at the others, recognizing none. Like Uncle Lao Weng, their faces were colorless. Clothes, too, were the color of bleached bone. At a distance, they'd looked to be wearing white, but this close to them, he could tell the whiteness derived from their state.

Lao Weng bowed. "We'll gladly take your tangerines, Tân, and anything else you may have to offer. We're hungry," he said, eyeing the fruit. "Hungry like we've not eaten in decades."

Tân said, "But why would you hunger, Uncle, when the village always provides for the ghosts?"

Lao Weng smiled and raised a hand to Tân's shoulder, turning him to face toward home. "It's hard to visit on the holy days when one is trapped in a reincarnation engine, nephew," he said, patting Tân across his shoulders with a hand that felt suspiciously solid for that of a ghost—solid, yet, soft and... *gummy,* as though it lacked bones, and perhaps skin, but held substance, nonetheless.

🦇 🦇 🦇

The reincarnated souls sat at his table, crowded together shoulder to shoulder, eating sticky rice balls, a bit of fish and more tangerines.

Heng scurried from table to stove, unsmiling, filling bowls, splashing water into cups, and hovering nearby, frowning at the mess they made of her house.

In the light, the ghosts were harder to see, a paleness against the luminance of day. In the place where they might once have had a belly hovered the consumed food they slurped and gobbled, a dark mass against the paleness. But they had no flesh to keep it in.

When Lao Weng reached for his third tangerine at the table, the action of bending at the waist extruded a glop of the masticated repast onto the dirt floor of the home. As if they didn't notice, the visitors continued to eat.

Tân looked at Heng with raised eyebrows. She shrugged back, the most minimal raise of shoulders as if not to draw attention to herself. Tân cleared his throat. "Uncle," he said, "I am honored to serve you in this life, but I am curious...?"

Lao Weng looked up from his plate, smiling. "I know what you want to know," he said, reaching for another tangerine and turning back to the meal at hand. Between bites he said, "I didn't know when I gave my soul up to the reincarnation engine that the possibility even existed for me to return to this earth as *me.*" He reached for a cup of water, lifted it quickly to his mouth, drank, and sat it back down again. "I am not the ghost of your ancestor, Tân, I am your ancestor, back to life, reincarnated in the engine, rather than the Tao."

Heng backed away from the table. Tân felt himself longing to do so as well. Not the ghost of his ancestor? But not really his ancestor. Then what? And how long did Uncle Lao Weng intend to stay?

🦇 🦇 🦇

Tân crossed the wooden bridge to the temple and rang the bamboo chime to request an audience with the priests. His face and hands felt the cold of the day, but he was warm from the hike. Only a moment passed before the rice-paper door slid open a fraction to admit him. Heat rolled out the door, warming his face.

Tân bowed. "I need an exorcism," he said.

Hu stepped back to admit Tân, then closed the door behind him.

"Perhaps you would like to pray first?" Hu said. He reached for a mask.

"To whom?" Tân asked.

"To the ancestor you wish to exorcise?"

"I have no need to pray to him when he is in my home, consuming my profits, as easy to converse with as you."

The recitation did not seem to phase Hu. Had he seen this before, Tân wondered?

Hu bowed, sliding the mask to a small table. He turned away from Tân and lit some incense in a small brazier, then bowed over it. "Let's talk of this exorcism," he said.

🦇 🦇 🦇

As head priest, Sheng performed the exorcism. She carried a mirror, etched with the eight spiritual trigrams around the edge, the symbols for sky, earth, water, fire, thunder, wind, mountain and lake, and led the way to Tân's house.

Hu carried a chicken and the ceremonial knife with which to slit its breast. Li brandished a staff with eight cross-arms at the top, each holding eight brass bells engraved with the eight trigrams. Tân pulled a cart containing six earthenware jars, one for each spirit invading his home.

The priests approached Tân's house, ringing the bells, flashing the mirror and chanting the exorcism ritual.

Lao Weng stood on the raised wooden porch as they arrived and said, "An exorcism! What ghosts do we banish today?" He smiled open-mouthed and Tân could count the wood grains on the weathered door of his house through Lao Weng's gaping maw. He felt the gorge rise up his throat, but forced it down. He could be brave with the priests here to help.

"Lao Weng." Sheng bowed. "We come to remove you and your friends. Would you be so kind as to enter the jar yourself?

Tân removed the first jar from the cart and set it on the spot Sheng indicated.

Lao Weng laughed. "You cannot exorcise me," he said. "I am not a spirit." He walked down the steps holding a hand out to Sheng. "Feel me. Trust what your hands touch if you can't believe what your eyes see."

Sheng swung her hand in an arc as though she thought it would pass through Lao Weng's. It slapped against his, pushing it away.

He smiled. "See? Flesh. I am alive."

"Not quite," said Sheng, looking down at her palm, rubbing her thumb across the pads of her fingers, "but neither are you a ghost. You are... in between."

She turned to Tân. "Pack up the jars."

"But the exorcism?" Tân asked.

"We can't help with unwanted guests," Sheng said.

A strangled cry from the porch had them all turning to Heng.

She rushed forward, *click, click, click,* and struck one of the half-reincarnated spirits in the back.

He flew off the porch, landing in the dirt by Sheng's feet. His flesh ripped, leaving a slit large enough for the soul to escape. A whining keen erupted from the tear.

Sheng reached for her mirror and motioned for Tân to open the nearest jar.

Vapor, like steam from a kettle, hissed from the reincarnated corpse. Sheng held the mirror above it, and with expertise learned from years of practice, rebounded the escaping soul into the jar.

Tân slammed down the lid.

Chanting, Li rang bells over the jar. Hu wrung the neck of the chicken and gutted it, then marked the jar with blood. Sheng dropped the mirror and with intricate hand motions, performed the *mudra* necessary to seal the soul within.

Heng stared in open-mouthed horror from the porch, but quickly snapped from her stupor. She rushed forward again and shoved the four remaining souls from the porch. Four more times, Sheng used the mirror to direct souls into earthenware jars.

Lao Weng said to Sheng. "You condone this?"

Sheng bowed. "I can neither condone nor not condone."

"But this is murder!" Lao Weng said.

"I'm not so sure," said Sheng, "since you are neither alive nor dead. I will meditate upon it." She turned to leave. "By custom, you are still welcome in Tân's home."

"And be murdered in my sleep?"

"Sleep?" interjected Tân, "You have not slept yet! All you do is eat, eat, eat."

"He is not welcome at your hearth?" Sheng asked, turning to Tân and lifting a brow.

Tân looked to Heng. With a negative shake, perhaps imperceptible to the others, she let Tân know her wishes. He would serve a special penance in the bureaucracy of hell for that, he knew, but he was willing. Heng gave him the courage.

"No," Tân said. "He is not welcome."

Sheng said to Lao Weng. "You may stay with us."

Tân's face burned with shame. What he was not willing to do, the priests would do in his place. He would have to increase his temple donations twice-over for them to keep up with Lao Weng's appetite.

Sheng said, "Load the jars back on the cart. Lao Weng–" she turned to him, raising her left arm in a gesture of fellowship, "join me, please. We will walk together."

"It is a trick!" Lao Weng said, stumbling backward and rushing headlong up the stairs toward Heng.

Fear covered Heng's face. She ran to the door of the house.

Lao Weng hurdled up the remaining steps and *leapt* into Heng's body. His pale, boneless self sank beneath Heng's tanned flesh and disappeared.

Heng screamed and ran back and forth on the porch, jumping and flailing as Lau Weng sought control of her body.

Tân knew the instant his Uncle won: Heng quieted, and the peaceful light in her eyes turned to triumph. The voice was Heng's but the words were Lao Weng's: "See what comes of denying your ancestor his due, Tân?" Lao Weng laughed, Heng's eyes squeezed closed like Tân remembered his uncle's used to do.

When they were little, he and his cousins had called the laughing Lao Weng *piggy*, with his squinting eyes and big cheeks. And a pig is what he had become, in death, if not in life. Tân's hand itched to slap the satisfied look from Lao Weng's face. How shameful, that his Uncle desired life so much that he would steal someone else's.

Anger seared his chest.

"Can you do nothing, now?" Tân asked Sheng. "Surely Heng is not dead?" Tân felt his heart catch. Tears scalded his eyes. He had not thought of that possibility until just now.

"She's not dead," said Sheng, and Tân felt himself relax. "Lao Weng has pushed her aside and taken over her body."

"But you can remove him," Tân said.

Sheng nodded. "I can."

"Then do so!"

"This is an unusual exorcism," Sheng said. "The astrology

must be exactly right. We must take care not to harm Heng's soul."

"Hurry," said Tân. "While we discuss it, Heng must abide that pig inside her skin."

Sheng bent to knock a bit of dust from the hem of her robe. "I must think," she said.

"I'll pay," Tân said. "Whatever you want, I'll pay. Now help her." He looked at Heng and saw only Lao Weng. He turned away, unable to bear the sight of him.

"Whatever I want?" Sheng said. "I want nothing."

"What will it take?" said Tân.

Sheng said, "You have two choices: Heng or no Heng. What would you pay to have Heng?"

Tân sank to his knees moaning, his hand pressed against his ears, his eyes tightly shut. "I'll do it," he said, dropping his hands and looking up. "I pledge my soul to the engines." His voice became flat. "Now please save Heng."

Sheng said, "Only your willingness is required. You may yet have your wish and avoid the engines." She nodded at Hu.

Hu tightened his grasp on the ceremonial knife. He sped to Heng, vaulting onto the porch, and sank the blade hilt-deep into her right shoulder.

Tân looked on with horror, the event happening so quickly, he couldn't voice his denial. Heng staggered, the wooden treads of her shoes thudding unevenly on the porch as she appeared to search for balance. Her face paled, and she sank back against the wall of the house, supported by Hu.

The edges of her figure blurred and Lao Weng pitched forward, peeled from her body. He somersaulted off the porch, landing in the dirt on his back. At his right shoulder, a hole gaped in the whiteness of his flesh. No blood poured forth.

As if unwilling to shed the skin it so recently wore, Lao Weng's soul took long moments to exit the wound. Only slender, tentative curls of vapor exited the slash. Sheng lifted the bells at her waist in one hand and her mirror in the other. Baiting the soul, she shook the bells in an intricate pattern, their brass intonations dull in the humid afternoon.

Like a moth to flame, Lao Weng's soul swooped through the hole and battered into Sheng's mirror.

Tân waited, lid poised open over the last empty jar.

Lao Weng's soul caromed off the underside and slid helpless into the earthenware container. Tân slammed down the lid, then sank to his knees breathing deeply. He looked up at Sheng.

"I don't understand," he said. "You said you could do naught. Then there was talk of murder, and yet," he broke off and turned to Hu, pointing. "You came forward and—as if you had planned the taking of his soul."

Hu smiled, and Sheng looked as though she might like to. Pity, Tân thought, they couldn't hide behind their masks here.

Sheng said, "We had no plan other than exorcism when we came today," she said. "Opportunity presented itself when Lao Weng stole Heng's body. Hu knew exactly what to do. And so, your problem is solved. With your help, we shall return these souls to the temple so that they might be cleansed. Would you be interested in using them again?" she asked.

Tân shook his head. "No."

"But these souls have worked for you for years," she said. "They know what to expect of you, you know what to expect of them."

"I know more about these souls than I care to know."

Sheng nodded, then turned to Hu and Li who had begin the ritual binding of the corpses on shrouds of white. Tân could see that neither looked happy. He knew corpse binding provided little joy for anyone, but this task irritated more than most. As Li and Hu grasped the bodies by shoulder and ankle, the bodies ripped as easily as the flesh of the tangerines growing in the fields beyond his house.

He turned away. Heng bloodied and bandaged, watched tight-lipped from the porch. She would not leave, he knew, until all the bodies were gone.

Nonetheless, his heart felt light, as he loaded the jars onto the cart and began the journey back to the temple. He may eventually spend time in an engine, also perhaps in one of these very jars, but the rest of his family would not. He smiled. Good deeds cost nothing, but were more valuable than a lifetime of profits.

The Analytical Engine of Hester Watts, Grand Mistress of the Unseen

Laura Duerr

With a dramatic swish of silk scarves, I took my seat at the black-draped table. "Mrs. Horace, what brings you to my parlor this day?"

"Parlor" was a generous description for the séance chamber I'd built in the back of a steam lorry, but Mrs. Horace hardly noticed. She sniffled and dabbed her eyes with a lace-trimmed handkerchief, but even in the flickering candlelight I could tell her tears were feigned.

"Mistress Watts, my late husband–" Mrs. Horace broke into exaggerated sobs, at which point her son, a handsome young man perhaps a little younger than me, sat up with a sigh.

"My mother wishes to confer with the spirit of my father, Mr. Wesley Horace of Aerosphere Enterprises."

The younger Mr. Horace was clearly a skeptic. They were always more satisfying to impress than the believers. People like him needed to be convinced by a show unlike anything other mediums could provide, but I knew my Analytical Engine was up to the task.

It helped that today's client was the famous widow of an infamous aeronautics mogul. Mr. Horace's company was better known for its disastrous crashes than its innovative designs. Camden Town was abuzz with gossip about the Horaces, and their staff—particularly the son of their beleaguered driver—were more than willing to sell me a few of their secrets. My punch cards were ordered like cues in a symphony to address any possible question the widow and son might ask, from illegitimate children to corporate secrets.

It also helped that most of London had not yet heard that Hester Watts, Grand Mistress of the Unseen, was a fraud. My mobile séance parlor made keeping ahead of my rapidly deteriorating reputation as simple as topping up the boiler. The rarefied circles so obsessed with spiritualism enjoyed the slightly scandalous detour to my quaint workplace, while the constant hiss of the lorry's steam engine gave them a sense of privacy. It never occurred to them that the engine could be powering a computational machine that would impress Babbage and Lovelace themselves.

"His passing is a great loss," I said, nodding solemnly beneath my scarves. "Should Mr. Horace answer us today, what do you wish to ask?"

Mrs. Horace took a trembling breath. "It's just—he had an assortment of precious gems, very fine treasures acquired during his travels in India. But it seems only he knew where they are, and I—I wish to find them, for they were my darling husband's, and they're ever so dear to me—"

Another wealthy widow utilizing a medium in order to obtain more wealth—how unoriginal. I'd already worn out my welcome in America, but here, in the land of my birth, I could find innumerable bereaved aristocrats willing to pay so the deceased could tell them about airship stocks, or secret caches of wealth, or whether Cousin So-and-So was *really* the intended beneficiary of the estate. The whole business was exasperating, but soon, I'd have enough for passage to Australia. There, unlike in Britain or even the States, no one would turn his nose up at a female engineer. Besides, the weather was ever so agreeable.

"I shall attempt to contact him. Be still, please."

Concealed by the table, I fed a series of punch cards from my skirts into a slot in the lorry's false wall. The hisses and clanks of my Analytical Engine were muted by the insulated walls; still, I raised my voice as I called upon the spirits.

"Mr. Wesley Horace! Your bereaved wife and son seek you. Will you speak with them?"

Right on time, a small drum mounted above the lorry's false ceiling rapped two sharp beats. Mrs. Horace gasped. Even her son deigned to look interested.

"Wesley! Darling, is that you? Rap thrice if it's you!"

"Or play us a flute," the son muttered. I swiftly picked another card from my skirt and fed it into the machine's override slot. Switches clicked behind me, so softly only I would hear, as the Analytical Engine interrupted my initial set of programming instructions and rearranged its gears and springs to carry out its new orders. Three times the drum beat, and from another corner of the lorry, the wistful trill of a flute sounded.

The younger Mr. Horace now looked genuinely impressed. Mrs. Horace wasn't even pretending to cry anymore. "Wesley," she cried, "your gems, where are they? Give us a sign!"

The Analytical Engine ran through its series of cards, triggering levers and gears concealed behind the false walls, which in turn tapped on drums, twisted creaky boards, and ignited gas lamps within hidden projectors. An image materialized on the wall next to us: a rectangle of color suggesting a generic landscape.

"Do you recognize that painting?" I asked in a theatrical whisper.

"That dreadful Dutch landscape in his office!" Mrs. Horace gasped. "You loved that painting—of course you'd hide your treasures behind it!"

The Analytical Engine gave a final drumroll. A hidden valve extinguished the candles on the table. I slumped and let my scarves fall across my face, pretending to be overcome. In truth, I was practically beaming with pride. I'd built an Analytical Engine by myself from scrounged gears and wires—and made it mobile, no less—and it was as reliable as a rooster. Maybe I ought to stay in London and submit it to some stodgy scientific board, if only to see the reactions on their mustachioed faces.

"Your husband was most eager to help you, Mrs. Horace," I said weakly. "He wants you to be happy—"

Mrs. Horace was already on her feet, rummaging among her ample skirts for her purse. She dropped the whole thing on the table.

"Thank you, Mistress Watts," she said. "You've saved our family legacy!" She dabbed at her eyes again, though they were still dry. There would certainly be tears later, though, once she'd tossed the priceless Dutch landscape aside and destroyed the wall in search of gems that weren't there. I felt no remorse; the family legacy would remain as gilded as ever.

"It is my pleasure," I said, plucking the purse from the table. The son cast an appraising glance over his shoulder as he escorted his mother down the lorry steps into the sunny morning. I had indeed managed to impress him—and he was quite handsome, not to mention wealthy, gems or no. Too bad I'd have to leave Camden Town before getting the opportunity to know him better. I closed up the lorry behind them.

I cycled out the punch cards and filed them away in their box. The walls were only slightly warm; apparently I'd successfully fixed the overheating problem that had almost given me away in Bath. I pried off a few wall panels to make sure the gears were still well-oiled—in particular, the rapid-fire rotations required to power the drumroll were especially taxing. Everything seemed to be in order, though, from the assorted landscape slides on their rotating wheel to the rubber seams that muffled the hiss and clank of the Analytical Engine.

With my post-appointment checks complete, I clambered

into the lorry's cab and let myself out through the driver's door. I'd parked a discreet distance from Regent's Park so as not to alarm any of the residents taking the morning air; other than the four-legged automatons trimming the grass, no one was around to see a young woman dressed in spangly black scarves jump down from a hissing steam lorry. I rolled up the painted canvas signs hanging on the lorry's sides that advertised my trade. It was a lovely morning; the foxglove trees were in full flower and the garden beds bloomed a riot of color that reminded me of the wildflower fields of my childhood.

I climbed back into the driver's seat and allowed myself a moment to watch the gleaming, dog-sized automatons as they trundled among the flowers. The sight filled me with longing. I tried to tell myself it was because of the beautiful automatons, and not the nostalgia the flowers stirred in my heart.

Before I could fall too deeply into introspection, I put the lorry in gear and drove down to Camden Lock. There were automatons here, too, considerably larger and more tarnished models that handled cargo and pulled carts. The clamor was deafening compared to the reserved hush of the park: traders, fishmongers, housewives, street vendors, and house help all mingled in the crowded market alleys. The air was thick with steam and redolent of canal water, coal, and sweat. Despite the commotion, I felt more at home here than I ever did in the tidy parks where I saw my clients. Here, I could go unnoticed, just another person trying to make her way. I felt pleasantly invisible, even in my ridiculous Mistress of the Unseen garb.

I navigated carefully past other lorries and steam carriages and parked alongside the canal. Almost immediately, a pair of kitchen maids out doing the shopping hurried to my window.

"What'd you tell her?" one of them asked breathlessly.

"She'll be tearing holes in the walls of her husband's study by time you get back."

They grinned at each other. "The master'll be most upset. He's got gambling debts like his father—probably wanted the gems to pay his off, too."

"Such a shame, isn't it?" I pressed coins into their waiting palms. "Some of that is for Roger, the driver's son—his commission, you might call it."

"Pleasure doing business," the maid giggled, tucking her payment inside her coat. "I assume you've heard about Lord Owens losing his grandfather?"

I perked up. "Why, no, I haven't." Another coin slipped out the window into her hand.

"Called him the Old Cannon, they did," she continued. "When he drank too much—"

"Which was every time, to hear tell," added the other.

"—he'd go off like a cannon. Awful, he was, to upstairs and downstairs alike."

"But the grandson?" I asked. "Lord Owens?"

"Cannon the Third," the maid said, her lip twisting. "Only he don't have to be drunk."

I gave them each another coin. "You've been most helpful. If you're in touch with anyone at the Owens household—"

"We'll send them your way." The maids nodded and stepped away, blending so seamlessly with the crowd that I lost them in mere moments.

I started up the lorry's engine and returned to Regent's Park. My afternoon appointment wasn't due for another hour, but the Analytical Engine had to be ready to impress, and I had condolences to write to this Lord Owens.

But three people—a man and two women, one dressed in black —were waiting for me when I returned my lorry to its usual place. The sight inspired a flash of panic: it was far too early for my next appointment, and the last time I had a crowd waiting for me was when Edinburgh discovered my secret and ran me out of town.

I parked the lorry and disembarked with as much grace as one disembarking in petticoats from a very high lorry seat could muster. Before I could greet the visitors, the young man, who couldn't have been older than 20, hurried up to me.

"Mistress Watts?"

"Yes?"

"Please, we don't have an appointment, but I need your help."

"I am sorry," I said regally, "I have another appointment within the hour—"

"It's my husband." The woman in black, her round face blotchy from weeping, pushed forward. The other woman followed closely. They looked alike—sisters, I judged, the one in black several years younger.

"Your husband?"

"He died." She stood taller, her chin set defiantly as if she expected me to mock or belittle her grief. "Frederick is—was—" Her voice wavered, but she gripped her sister's hand and continued. "He was a merchant. His airship was lost over the Indian Ocean and no one will tell me—"

Her resolve finally broke and she dissolved into sobs in her sister's arms. The sister rubbed her back and whispered something to her; the young man looked helpless. I thought I must look just as dumbfounded as he, and was grateful for my veil: I'd never seen such a genuine displays of grief from my customers.

I'd also never had customers quite so shabby. The young man looked reasonably well-off, but the widow and her sister wore no jewelry, and their dresses were several years out of style. They'd clearly tried to keep up appearances, but the fabrics were worn and patched in places. The widow still wore a ring, a thin gold band, but the sister's pale fingers showed no signs of ever bearing one.

It crossed my mind that these people would not be able to pay me well; that thought was immediately eclipsed by annoyance that they might inconvenience my upcoming, and no doubt wealthier, client. I shoved both uncharitable reactions away. Pieces were beginning to click together: the poor girl had married for love, to a man below her station, and subsequently suffered her family's disapproval, or else the parents had died and left them nothing. Her maiden sister, perhaps, had supported the match, and in turn been supported by the deceased merchant.

"When did he die?" I asked.

"Nearly two years ago," she whispered. "I know it's a long time to be mourning, but if I only had answers, perhaps..." She glanced briefly at the young man, who looked back at her with tenderness. She took a deep breath and slipped the wedding ring from her finger.

"We can pay," she said, holding it out.

My hand twitched forward. Even a modest ring like hers was worth enough to send me to Australia in style.

"We can discuss that after," I managed. "Come in."

I ushered them inside the lorry's parlor. They arranged themselves around the table while I lit candles. The stack of programming cards thumped against my leg as I navigated the crowded space.

"What are your names?"

"I'm Richard Weaver, and this is my best friend's widow, Mrs. Emmeline King, and her sister, Miss Eudora Conroy."

I seated myself and began to secretly pull cards from their pouch. "How did you know the deceased?"

"I've known Fred since we were boys. We were schoolmates."

"Mr. Weaver was our best man," Emmeline added, smiling at him through her tears, though Richard wouldn't look up from the table.

"And then I got him the job that killed him," Richard said. "I have contacts at Aerosphere Enterprises, and Fred thought a job on an airship sounded jolly exciting."

"It isn't your fault," Emmeline whispered. "We keep telling him it isn't his fault, don't we, Eudora?"

"It isn't, Mr. Weaver, darling," Eudora said.

How curious that another appointment should connect to Aerosphere Enterprises and their cheap airships. I felt even more vindicated in leading Mrs. Horace to vandalize her own home.

Richard finally looked up and met Emmeline's eyes.

"We'll have our answers soon," she whispered.

More pieces clicked together. I began feeding cards into the

Analytical Engine. It hummed to life like the opening of a sonata.

"He comes," I whispered. Small vents made the candles flicker. Something hidden in a corner knocked softly; crumpling paper mimicked the sound of the ocean.

"Do you hear that?" Richard was watching Emmeline avidly. I saw tears standing in his eyes.

"The seashore." She gazed back at him. Eudora still gripped her hand, but her watchful gaze was fixed on me, not her.

Richard looked up at the ceiling. "Freddy, tell us—tell us what happened."

Shrieking metal. Emmeline covered her mouth with her free hand. Richard made as if to reach for her, but stopped.

I closed my eyes. "An accident, he says—a storm. The rudder snapped off and they were driven into the sea."

Emmeline sobbed and this time Richard seized the sisters' clasped hands. Eudora gently extricated hers. She was still watching me, her gaze meaningful in a way I believed I understood. She, too, was a skeptic—but her sister and Richard believed, and that was what mattered.

I fed a trio of fresh cards into the machine. My watch hung next to the pouch of cards, but I resisted the urge to glance at it —I'd be finished with these clients in time for my next appointment, but even if I wasn't, he'd just have to bloody wait.

"Mr. King wishes you to know that retribution has come to Aerosphere Enterprises," I said. It was only slightly true, but they would have known that Mr. Horace had died—indeed, the occasion might have triggered Emmeline's desire for closure—and in a few day's time, certain society papers would almost certainly regale their readers with the tale of the bereaved Mrs. Horace's madness. "He says, 'Do not carry bitterness or vengeance in your heart, my beloved.'"

I'd chosen my words purposefully, and watched as Richard's face fell and his grip loosened on the word 'beloved.'

The sound of the surf resumed, and a wave of rosy perfume wafted across the table. "He is glad you summoned him," I told Emmeline. "He misses you."

"And I, him." But she was watching Richard's face, crestfallen.

"His wish now is only for your happiness; you are young and beautiful, and you mustn't waste the rest of your days in mourning."

"I've missed him so terribly..."

"Of course you have. You had so little time together—but now you can treasure that time and carry the memory with you. And you, Mr. Weaver—" I tilted my head, as if listening. The sound of the surf ended. "He, too, insists this is not your fault, and says he knows your heart is true and loyal, and that you will know what that means."

Richard finally looked up at Emmeline. She gave a half-smile, a small gesture laden with hope.

"I think I do," he said.

The last cards cycled through the machine, producing a wistful trill of flute music and a fresh breath of roses. No dramatic drumroll or extinguishing candles were needed. Emmeline covered Richard's hand with her own.

I sank back in my chair and spoke with feigned exhaustion. "I hope you found the answers you sought."

"I did," Emmeline said.

For the first time since they'd arrived, Richard smiled. "*We* did."

Eudora was the first to stand; I had the impression she'd been waiting months for her sister and their friend to let go of their guilt. Emmeline and Richard stood together, their hands still clasped across the table.

"Mistress Watts has another appointment," Eudora reminded them gently.

"Of course." Richard released Emmeline, who let her sister lead her out of the lorry while still gazing over her shoulder at Richard.

"Mistress Watts, thank you—you have no idea—Oh!" She stopped suddenly and removed the ring again. "Here. Your payment."

"Keep it," I said. "This was very much my pleasure."

Richard took a worn leather purse from his jacket pocket. It did not look heavy. "At least let us donate something—"

Having to refuse payment a third time was becoming challenging to my character. I did not appreciate the sensation, but I appreciated even less the character I'd have if I took money from these people. "Consider this a gift towards your future happiness," I said.

He stowed the purse reluctantly. "We very much appreciate it. Thank you—from both of us."

Eudora led her sister from the lorry. Richard paused and turned back. "I've never really put much stock in this spiritualism stuff. Was it true? Did he really say all that?"

Had any of my other clients asked, I might have acted affronted, or mystically reassured them that yes, the spirits had spoken such, and you'd do well to heed them. Part of me still hastened to defend my reputation and swear it had all been real —but not only was my professional exposure imminent, I couldn't bring myself to lie to this young man any more than I already had, after the months of heartache he'd surely endured. After all, if someone had been so honest to me back in my days of wildflower fields, I'd have been saved a very different kind of heartache.

"Does it matter?" I said. "Your hearts already know the truth."

He thought for a moment, then nodded once and left the lorry. I wondered if he would ever tell Emmeline, or if she had suspicions of her own. At the end of the day, though, I'd done what any savvy medium, fraudulent or no, seeks to do: tell their customer what they want to hear. If Emmeline and Richard went on to live happily ever after, and Eudora was taken care of, it would feel even more rewarding than all my years of swindling the crooked and malicious. I found I was quite glad I hadn't taken their payment.

I let the candles burn. The smoke would add to the atmosphere for my next appointment, and the light was enough to pen a letter to Lord Owens. Cannon the Third, I vowed, would be my final client in London. After setting him to rights, my Analytical Engine and I would be off to Australia, where surely more of the crooked and malicious—but also the heartbroken and grieving—awaited us.

THE THOUSAND INJURIES
ERIC CLINE

I sat in silence as my old friend, my father-in-law, made his confession.

After he had finished, he sat back in his chair, with that sad smile on his face. And there was silence.

Silence? Not after that. I could not bear it.

"Fifty years?" I said. Fifty years ago he had committed this crime? Before Italy had become a united country? Before he had married? Before my wife had been born?

He nodded. The smile never left his face.

I got up and left his study.

"I think I shall..." but could not utter anything more of an excuse. My father-in-law waved his hand indulgently.

This was not a place of murder, surely.

It was night in his ancestral home. Servants walked about here and there, intent on their tasks, not making eye contact. The oil lamps, which had replaced the torches of a generation ago, suffused the high ceilings with a glow. Tapestries hung on the walls, keeping the solid stones of this old palazzo from radiating their coldness. No, not this lovely home. Upstairs, my wife, fatigued by our long journey to visit her father, slept in comfort. This was not a place of murder.

Surely.

But then my eyes alit upon a certain set of archways, at the end of which lay a heavy oaken door. The path he claimed to have led his victim through.

My father-in-law is very old. Senility? Perhaps not. He was always a prankster. The Italians are known for their *joie de vivre*–not that he would appreciate an Austrian son-in-law applying a French term to it! Perhaps, perhaps he had not gone feeble-minded so much as his taste in jokes had deteriorated. Yes, that could be!

So. He could be in his second childhood. Or this could just be an extended joke, ill-advised.

Surely, there had been no murder here.

Yet, my feet were moving of their own accord.

I took an oil lamp with me. I opened the door. Its creak could be heard throughout the ground floor. I imagined him grinning, as his arthritic body rested in the chair.

Fooled the lad. Ha ha! A great jest indeed.

I had been down here once, briefly. I had seen the bones. Of his ancestors. Of my wife and children's ancestors. It had been a brief visit, barely beyond the bottom of the steps. But it had been enough.

I closed the door behind me carefully. There was no snap lock, just a bolt which could never accidentally latch. Still, I fanned the door a couple of times just to reassure myself. Then I made my way down.

They were spiral steps. I went slowly in case of some mossy slipperiness. This was a damp place. Patches of nitre grew freely.

At mid-way, the door had disappeared around the bend from above, and the land-ing had not yet appeared below. I almost hastened my pace. Almost. But I am a Viennese man, not superstitious, and of good nerve. I let myself stay in this purgatory between the world above and the world below. If my breath quickened, if my throat bobbed with a heavy gulp, that was not to my discredit. I did not run as a scared boy.

The "reliquary," as it were, began almost immediately. Italy became a modern 19th century nation in the decade after my father-in-law's (supposed!) crime. The newer villas built after Garibaldi's armies united Italy, kept only wine in their cellars, and the dead were exiled to sensible cemeteries. But the old families, like the one I had married into, still kept their dead with them. As I walked along I saw bones covered with the rotted threads of shrouds, on both sides of me.

They moved. Of course they did. The shadow from my lamp gave them that illusion as I walked along. I had steeled myself for it. I don't share the sentimentality or the superstition of Italians —or the rural Aus-trian mountainfolk. In between the skeletons stacked seven-deep along the walls, incongruous enough almost to be a joke by themselves, were casks of wine. The area was well-swept and well-trod. Servants came down, at least this far, on a regular basis. The assistant cook, on some other day, might brush past her master's great-great-grandparents to get him a good port to go with his dinner.

It was all too ridiculous. I am formally Catholic, but this outdated, morbid tradition is abhorrent to me. That was why I did not laugh.

That was why.

This was a place filled with generations of dead.

But murder?

Well, down here, it seemed still unlikely. But not preposterous.

A rat scurried past me, a few feet away.

It startled me. But then the crazy thought came unbidden: was it running away from *me,* or...?

Damn me, I looked behind me. Only the bones, seven-deep, of my wife and children's ancestors.

"I am the only thing here," I thought. "That little animal ran from *me.*" But I had not thought it. I had said it aloud. And I could not hear myself.

These catacombs sucked out all traces of human life. Voices. Flesh. No wonder they were where bodies were left to desiccate, and wine was safely preserved.

Further I went, beyond where servants usually came. I could not believe that these tunnels stretched under the entirety of the ancestral home and grounds. Surely this place could not stretch all the way out underneath the river? There was talk in the papers of electricity coming to us soon. I tried to imagine those magical wires and glass bulbs being installed in a place like this. No. It would never do. Oil and water. The past and the future could not coexist.

The floor became gritty under my shoes. I knew that no servants trafficked this far in.

The catacomb bent. I followed, a sleepwalker from a future century, who, barely an hour before, had been discussing the recent spate of sensational British novels with my father-in-law, when he had decided to reminisce. *'You, who so well know the nature of my soul...'* he had begun, in a friendly tone, and had proceeded to narrate his grisly 'confession.' No, I had not known! How could my world up-end that quickly?

I had earlier disliked the illusion of a purgatory on the winding stone steps; now that illusion was redoubled as I found myself standing in my own little patch of lamplight, in nothing, with nothing behind me and nothing ahead.

The *illusion.* Yes, that was it.

I felt an icicle trail down my forehead. It was sweat, made

chilly in this place.

How foolish! To go down here on the vaguest whim. Above me, though I could not hear them, servants still went about their duties. My father-in-law lazed in his chair. A few floors above that, my wife slept, and fully expected me to come and warm the bed.

There could be no terror, in a place encompassed within the ancestral palazzo.

The grandfather of my children was not a murderer, and his victim could not be interred here.

Could not. Illusion. Glass. I had just stepped on glass?

No, it wasn't glass. It was the faint jingling of a bell.

I forgot the cold. I forgot the world one flight of steps above me. Out of the dark gray of bones and stone, there came into relief moving patterns, like the heavy tubes of wind chimes in their slow drift. And though lamplight made color difficult to distinguish, some were red, some were white, some were black, or maybe the black was mere air in between patches of red and white. The jingling stopped and started, stopped and started, and within that short space of time coalesced the figure of a man, dressed in fool's motley, holding a bottle. It strained toward me as if bound by invisible chains.

"He ha! Are you back? I knew this was just some jest on your part!"

The words came to my ears, but did not seem to match the movements of the figure's mouth. I was reminded of a magic lantern show I had at-tended in which faint images appeared on a silk screen whilst a performer narrated what the characters were supposed to be saying.

"I do not know you," I said, barely above a whisper.

"Oh, you jest again, my friend. Come, let me loose! We shall laugh about this as we stroll the piazza and show off our costumes for Carnival."

The figure in fool's motley took a pull from the bottle in the middle of his words. Its bon-vivant hail-fellow gestures were overdone, as if for the stage.

"I cannot free you," I said, or perhaps thought. "It is far too late for that."

The Fool hung its head in dejection. Then lunged at me.

It was too swift for me to do more than flinch. But was held back by its invisible bindings. It could not pull away from that patch of wall, which was of slightly different pattern than the sections on either side.

"Ah well! Ha ha!" An exaggerated shrug and another pull on the bottle. "Well, it was the perfect prank. And you may let me loose, old friend, and we shall laugh about this. My wife expects me to join her tonight at Carnival, you know."

"I'm afraid you missed that appointment long ago," I muttered, and backed away from it, never letting it get out of my sight.

"For the love of God, my friend!" it wailed. "For the love of God!"

The Fool sagged in a posture of defeat. Red and white were fading back into gray stone. I risked turning my back to it, and ran headlong.

"For the love of God!" it shouted. And then a final, desperate cackle.

Running up the steps was the work of moments. I practically jumped at the door, in case I needed to force it open, but it was unlocked. And then I was back upstairs, in the world of reality. I extinguished the oil lamp and sat it on the nearest flat surface for some servant to deal with.

As I strode past the old man's study, where I had expected innocent conversation a lifetime and two hours ago. He looked up from a news-paper. He merely smiled at me, the old pirate.

I took the stairs two at a time, caring nothing for the wide-eyed look a maid going in the opposite direction gave me.

Not soon enough, but very soon, I had joined my wife in bed. She barely stirred, but snuggled next to me, like a vine entwining itself with a trellis.

I let her sleep. And I tried to as well. I was back in the world of the concrete. Of the all-seeing Catholic God. Of tradition and family and civilization. Of *harmless* ribald jest.

That night and a thousand nights after, I would try to tell myself that it was all some odd dream. Or that my father-in-law had hired a performer to hide in the catacombs and play sport with me.

But in truth, I would always know that poor Fortunato lurked below, still expecting to be led to a cask of Amontillado.

ONLY GUTTER GIRLS AND RUINED THINGS

JULIA K. PATT

Lidah didn't know how the clockwork cat came to be by their front stoop. It was too fine a thing for Mud Hollow with its glass eyes and its polished brass gears and its perfect rose quartz heart, nestled among the gleaming, ticking metal. The artisan had even jointed the tail so that it could thrash like a real cat's tail, and its wire whiskers bristled in the noonday light. Every now and then, it trilled, a high chiming note she imagined must be a meow.

Could be it had fallen from a passing carriage, she supposed, if its little master (or mistress) went careless at the wrong moment. Could be someone had tried to take it from the pretty little shop in River City and it got loose. Could be a crate had fallen from the cargo train that went through Thursday nights, calling its long mournful cry to the stars. Always woke her up, that train, and it was a trick not to knock her head on pantry shelves when she did.

Getting awful tall, Uncle Bart had said a few days back, and scratched his thick auburn beard in a way that worried her. Best not to bother Uncle Bart, especially when he was home from the mine and tired. Best not be too tall or eat too much or breathe too loud if Uncle Bart was tired. Of course, better him than Uncle Nolan. Best if Uncle Nolan never noticed her—or anyone.

Uncle Nolan had noticed the clockwork cat, though, and there was nothing to be done about it.

The first rock went wide, on account of the fact Nolan was already weaving on his feet and red-eyed and belching clouds of burning fumes. Lidah knew he could still be dangerous this way, though; he could still snag a wrist or a handful of hair if he wanted. Quick-fingered even when he was stewed was Uncle Nolan.

The second stone found its mark, though, dinging against one of the cat's perfect swiveling ears and leaving a sizeable dent. Another cracked one of its green glass eyes. Lidah flinched. She crouched by the side of the house; if she stayed quiet, Uncle Nolan wouldn't notice she was there.

But the hail of stones soon bored him; they could only leave scratches and dings and nicks in the polished metal. Out came the pistols, then, the pair of mother-of-pearl handled six-shooters Nolan carried at his hips. With these he never missed. The cat's back right leg buckled when the bullet hit its knee-joint. Another shot split that perfect thrashing tail in two. A third crushed its front left shoulder. Even Uncle Nolan couldn't shatter the rose quartz heart, though, not with its protective metal plating, and after a couple tries, he snarled in frustration, advanced on the little automaton, and stomped it into the dust under his boots.

All through it, the cat didn't make a noise, and that was worst of all.

Lidah leaned against the house, trying not to breathe, as Nolan returned to his spot on the porch and splayed loose-limbed back into his rocking chair. She waited an hour for his snores to settle into their steady, even drone. Then she scooped up the remains of the cat and scuttled back into the shadows.

The tinker-witch lived a mile out of town, by a little trickle of creek that was too small to be any use for panning. The water was useful for tinkering, though, because the witch kept a small forge running out behind her shack. It was there Lidah found her when she could finally get away from her chores and minding Uncle Nolan.

Neighbor folks said he was making a ruckus in the street. Uncle Bart had chastised her. What was that about now?

It was nothing, Lidah mumbled. *Just an old tomcat. Musta woke him up.*

Uncle Bart had only grunted.

She hid the cat under an old dress and behind the potatoes in the pantry. Although its quartz heart still ticked, the rest of it had been too badly damaged for it to move. The last few nights, she'd fallen asleep to its soft *clickclickclick*.

Now she cradled it as she approached the tinker-witch. A heavy mask hid the woman's face as she hammered at a piece of red-hot metal, shaping it into a plate, like a piece of armor. She heated and reheated it several times until she had worked it to her satisfaction and after, she etched intricate symbols on the interior side. Lidah stood, watching silently, throughout this process. Only when the tinker-witch pushed up her mask and demanded, "Well, what do you want?" did Lidah show her the broken remains of the clockwork cat.

The woman frowned at the mess. She was younger than Lidah had thought, with curly dark hair that sprayed out from either side of her face and freckles across her nose. Her eyes: green, like the cat's. Ash streaked her arms and clothes; she wore a man's heavy work boots. "Don't fix children's toys, 'specially them they broke on purpose. Ain'tcha a little old for that thing anyhow?"

"*I* didn't break it," Lidah said, sharper than she meant. "It were my unc and it weren't right he done it. It was just a pretty cat, not hurting no one. It don't deserve to be broke. I just want to fix it."

I just want to fix *something*, she didn't say.

The tinker-witch stripped off her gloves and took a big swig of water from a clay mug. She dragged one sooty forearm across her face, smearing her lips gray. "Got money?"

Lidah shook her head.

She scoffed. "Expect me to work for free, do you?"

"Thought you maybe could teach me how to fix it." Lidah toed the earth in front of her, not looking at the witch. "I can sweep and cook and warsh. And if you need things brought to and from the Hollow, could do that, too."

The tinker-witch folded her arms, considering. "Let me see it then," she said after a while, after Lidah was certain she'd say no.

She was a good tinkerer even if she was a witch; even Uncle Bart said so. When one of the automata broke in the mines, they always asked her to do the work, although only a few of them were brave enough to ask. Uncle Bart was brave enough, certainly.

She turned the cat over in her hands, clucking at the bullets and the dents. "Messed you up right good, didn't he?" she murmured to it.

To Lidah, she said, "Day after tomorrow, when the sky gets red. Bring a mop, 'cause I sure as shit ain't got one."

Lidah almost didn't get clear that first day; Uncle Nolan had lingered at the saloon and she couldn't leave the house with him still about. Not without earning Uncle Bart's ire and that she could not afford, cat or no cat, not when she lived off his charity. He liked to remind her of that, his charity. But it wasn't his fault her daddy'd run off to California or that her mama'd taken factory work up in Chicago, neither any sort of place for a child, they'd said. And wasn't it kind of her mama's brothers to take her in a while? Mama sent money and letters and city goods every month or so. Daddy had sent nothing since that first postcard from San Francisco.

No, she could not anger Uncle Bart.

So Uncle Nolan had been an unaccountably welcome sight that afternoon, lurching down the street like a brain-burned prairie wanderer. A jug hung loose from his trigger and middle fingers, and each time he stumbled, a little more sloshed out. By the time he reached the house, it had about all run out and he peered into the clay abyss as if pondering its mysteries. "'S'gone," he concluded and belched.

"C'mon, Unc, best you have some of your tea and lie down," Lidah said, coaxing him, from the porch. If she stayed out of reach, it was usually safe; sometimes it didn't even occur to him, it seemed, to pinch or slap at her if she wasn't too near him.

"Don't coddle me, girl." He stumbled toward her, almost tripping on the bottom step. "I'mma man grown, I am. Won't tolerate no kind of coddlin'."

"No, Unc," Lidah agreed. She walked backward into the house, while he followed like an unsteady toddler. "Only Uncle Bart says you must have your tea in the afternoons." *Put him to sleep, when you can,* Uncle Bart had told her more than once. *Keep him from hurting himself—or anyone else.*

Nolan batted at the air dismissively and almost lost his balance. "Oh, *hang* what Bart says." But this struck even him as blasphemy and he looked around as if expecting to see his brother frowning at him, disapproving.

When he finally staggered to bed, she flung an afghan over him, set his tea on the nightstand, and left his bucket by his bedside, should he wake up sick. His snores, big and buzzing, followed her out of town.

The clockwork cat lay in pieces on the tinker-witch's workbench. She'd drawn around them in white chalk to show how they had been configured. The broken pieces she'd laid out separate, and these she was considering when Lidah arrived, breathless. "First rule," the tinker-witch said without looking up. "Never take anything apart you can't put back together. That includes my house, young miss. Understand?"

Lidah nodded.

"Good. Now today. One clean kitchen for one list of parts we need and how to get 'em. Sound fair?"

It did—at least until she saw the tinker-witch's kitchen and the stack of dirty dishes stewing in black sink water. Cobwebs filled the cupboard, and a thick layer of dust stood upon the floor. Incongruously, a large brown splatter covered most of the ceiling.

"Ah, that," the tinker-witch said, leaning in the doorway. "Had a disagreement with some stew. And the mine foreman."

Even her uncles had never left the house in such a state. But a deal was a deal; Lidah tied up her hair in a kerchief and got to work. She went outside to pump fresh water, went to heat it on the hearth, thought better of it, and cleaned the cold stones of ash instead. Then she set about heating the water. She'd only gotten through the dishes when the tinker-witch interrupted her, laughing. "Okay, okay. That's enough for now. Let's have a look at your cat before the owl starts calling."

She showed Lidah the pile of parts that couldn't be repaired: several small springs and a few plates and two tiny shattered gears. "Easy enough to find or make, them," the tinker-witch explained. "The problem is this. Your winding mechanism's about split two. That uncle of yours 's a crack shot, he is."

He was famous for it once. First-rate gunslinger was our Nolan—before the drink got him, Lidah might have said. You should see him when he's sober. Except he never is anymore. Instead, she asked: "So what do we do?"

"Well," the tinker-witch said. "Can wait and see what turns up in the junk, then repurpose it for our use. That's what we'll do for the springs and the gears. Or...we steal it." Those green eyes regarded Lidah, steady, checking her reaction.

"Who from?"

The tinker-witch smiled.

Lidah couldn't sleep. She was curled in her usual space in the pantry, her head on the flour bag and her toes by the potatoes, her mother's quilt tucked around her like a cocoon. One of the uncles turned over in the other room and sighed. She felt like sighing herself but didn't dare. She felt quite sure if she made a noise or looked one of them in the eye, they would know. Uncle Bart, especially.

Tomorrow, she was going to steal from the mine.

The tinker-witch had given her a sharp, tapered tool for the job, something of her own invention. Just the right size and shape to pry open an automaton's back panel, under which she could find the winding mechanism.

We won't have the key, the tinker-witch had explained, *but it's easy enough to jury-rig 'em. There're folks back east make a very good living snatching clockwork.*

Like you? Lidah had asked.

The tinker-witch's eyes twinkled. *Now what makes you think that,* she said, rather than asked.

That's what makes you a tinker-witch, ain't it? How you spell machines and such?

She tossed her dark curls and laughed loud and long like a man. *Tinker-witch,* she repeated. *I like the sound of that.*

Little by little, Lidah had cleaned the tinker-witch's house. She'd scraped the dust from the old carpet, been surprised to find it red underneath. She washed all the linens and scrubbed all the floors. True, the *house* wasn't especially witchy, although it was quite dark and lonesome looking, with two windows like baleful eyes, sealed up with wax paper. The tinker-witch didn't own much that wasn't for tinkering. A few books, an oily bearskin, a map of the Dakota territories. She had a shiny silver pocket watch that Lidah had polished and a miniature portrait of a young woman with a sad smile. The tinker-witch hadn't explained, and Lidah hadn't asked.

The only place she hadn't cleaned was the little shed out back, which she figured was full of tinker-work or stolen goods or both.

Little by little, they had worked on the cat, too, and the tinker-witch had heated and reshaped the salvageable plates, knocked the dents and dings out with a tiny hammer and polished away the scratches with a rag. *Never get to do such dainty work anymore,* she told Lidah. *I was a clockmaker's apprentice once, you know. Back in Baltimore. 'Fore that I was a gutter girl, dirty as anything and mean as a rat and skinnier than you.*

It was the most she'd ever said about herself, and she looked as startled about it as Lidah. The tinker-witch shook her head.

Such a quiet one you are. Them uncles ever even hear you coming?

Lidah hadn't answered.

But now, they had put the cat most of the way back together, built it around its shining heart, still pulsing and lively. Lidah had dug the springs and gears out of the mine's junkyard, but there hadn't been anything like the winding mechanism.

Could always wait, the tinker-witch had said.

Could always just wait, Lidah told herself in the close quiet of the pantry. An uncle—Nolan most likely—snorted in his sleep. After all, it's just a toy for children. A pretty bit of nothing. No need to risk it.

Except Uncle Nolan had been getting drunker earlier—he'd come home before noon the other day and started a fight at the saloon two days later. It was getting so bad Uncle Bart was losing his patience, and when Uncle Bart lost his patience with Nolan, he lost his patience with Lidah, too. They were due for a blow-up. She could feel it, the same way she could feel storms creeping across the plains. And if she was honest, she didn't mean to be there when it happened this time.

It would be nice to have a friend, even a clockwork one, on the walk back East.

Lunch down at the mine happened dead at noon, so Lidah came right before the sun stood overhead and waited behind a fallen log. The men were milling around the mine entrance and among them were the automata: shining brass men who walked with sharp jerky movements and ticked and clicked as they went about their work. Their eyes were plain amber glass, but they still gleamed pleasantly in the sunlight. They came in all sizes, from as big as Uncle Bart to just two feet high, designed to fit in the smallest spaces to find the next vein. These littlest ones had the mechanism she needed; the others would be too large for the cat.

Some of the men were walking back to town to eat at home or have a quick pint at the saloon. She pressed her back against the log as they passed. If any of them looked back—

They didn't, happy enough to leave the mine behind them for the moment.

Lidah crept closer to the entrance. She could see Uncle Bart, easily identified with his red hair, standing halfway down the tunnel. Several feet away from him, closer to her, she could see one of the little automata, barely the size of a child, trundling towards the miners. It was her chance. Quick as she could, she dashed in and snatched up the machine. Only, it was heavier than she had imagined and she could only drag it out of the tunnel. She hadn't expected either, for it to make a noise, but it did, a small whistling alarm, just as she pulled it out of sight.

"What's that?" Uncle Bart thundered from within the tunnel.

She couldn't hear the response, but then he added: "Sounded like an automaton. The warning noise they make."

Were those footsteps approaching? She didn't have time to get away, so she pinned the twitching machine—it was trying to right itself—to the ground and worked the little pointed tool under the back panel. Slowly, oh too slowly, she unscrewed the edges of the winding mechanism and popped it from its setting. The automaton stopped moving immediately. Did its amber eyes look a little dimmer? Was its expression somehow sadder? Lidah swallowed the guilt welling up in her throat.

She did not look to see if Uncle Bart was coming. She only ran back up into the trees, slipping on dead leaves and sure she heard the sound of pursuit behind her.

The tinker-witch turned the mechanism over in her hands and murmured her approval. "This is good work, girl. You've barely scratched the edges. That's a light hand you have, even in a hurry."

It wasn't a perfect fit—the mechanism casing stood out half an inch from the cat's torso—but it went in well enough, and she was careful to show Lidah where the winding mechanism connected to the gears, how they caught on one another and then on more gears and how the whole thing turned and turned until it wound down. She fashioned a little wire key that Lidah slipped on a string around her neck. And the cat sprung up almost good as new.

There was still a little kink in its repaired tail, where it had been a perfect curve. And when it walked, one of the repurposed springs squeaked.

"Drop of oil will fix that," the tinker-witch assured her. Together they watched the cat stretch and pace and twitch its tail, and it regarded the two of them from its crystalline green eyes —although one was now just ordinary bottle glass.

That was right before Uncle Bart turned up.

Because it was Uncle Bart and he was unafraid—two tunnel collapses and both times he went in again and again until all the bodies were recovered—because of that, he came alone.

When the tinker-witch saw him crunching down the path, she shoved Lidah under the workbench. How did you know, Lidah wanted to ask. How did you know that was Uncle Bart? "Go on, you can sneak around the house and follow the path down the creek. There's a crossing, 'bout a half mile down. Go on and take this thing with you." She gestured at the cat, which Lidah took into her arms, cradling it as she scuttled away.

Uncle Bart was shouting before he even reached the tinker-witch. "You really dare to steal from me and mine?" he demanded. "Hasn't this town been good to you? Haven't we brought you trade? And here you steal from us, from the very thing that keeps us going." He spat.

It was just a little thing, Lidah wanted to say, hidden as she was on the other side of the witch's house. They had other automata. They would replace the box and the little machine would run again in a week or two.

The tinker-witch didn't offer any justifications. "You've no proof, Bart."

"I don't need proof," Bart hissed, so soft Lidah could barely hear him. He's furious, she wanted to warn the tinker-witch. He almost never talks that way. "One word from me and the good people of Mud Hollow would burn this dump to the ground."

"You won't, though," the tinker-witch replied. "Your mechanic ain't half as good as me."

A long ugly silence from Uncle Bart; Lidah almost *felt* him scowling. "Just give it back," he said.

"Can't give what I don't have."

Something—his fist—thudded on the workbench and there was a tinkle of colliding metal. "This is the fourth machine gotten tinkered this month. I'm giving you a chance, damn it."

"How generous," the tinker-witch replied, dryly.

Lidah was certain she would hear it then, the *whack* of her uncle's big fist hitting flesh, like the time he had struck Uncle Nolan for spending the grocery money on moonshine. But it was quiet, save for the sluggish gurgle of the creek next to her, and the soft whirring of the cat's gears.

Then: his boots rustling in the leaves as he stalked back up the path.

🦟 🦟 🦟

Lidah took the long way home. She hadn't wanted to go home at all, but the little sack of food and her coat and quilt were there. Not to mention mama's letters—they had her address in Chicago, the boarding house that wasn't fit for children. And if mama won't have me, she decided. I'll just be a gutter-girl like the tinker-witch until I can find some work. There were tinkerers in Chicago just as there were from New York to San Francisco. More automata, more tinkerers. And she was good at it, the tinker-witch had said so.

She was loath to sell the cat after it'd been such trouble to fix it up, but she could do that, too, find some wealthy, soft-eyed child who'd never been hungry or scared and sell the cat to its parents.

She came in the back through the kitchen and closed the clockwork cat in the pantry. It had almost wound down and she prayed it wouldn't make much noise while she waited for the uncles to fall asleep.

In the other room, Uncle Bart was raging.

"Lousy, good-for-nothing always piss-drunk—haven't done a damn day's worth of work in a year now. The hell's the matter with you, Nolan?"

Uncle Nolan was weeping, which was worst of all, because

nothing humiliated him like weeping in front of Uncle Bart. He cried on his own sometimes, like a child, and Lidah pretended she didn't hear. But Uncle Bart had beaten the man into him when they were younger, on account of granddaddy being dead so long before they grew up. Uncle Nolan hated crying in front of Uncle Bart; it made him feel small. Weak.

"You don't understand what it's like," he blubbered. "Weren't more than a *kid*, Bart, and I *shot* him. Shot him dead in the street." That had been before Lidah came, when Nolan was still a hired gun and the most famous shot in the territories.

Uncle Bart sighed. "It were an accident, Nolan," he said. His voice softer. Almost kind. "Everyone knows that."

"Still dead, ain't he." Nolan's voice split down the middle.

Bart didn't answer. Instead, he thundered her name, which was the worst sign of all. "LID*AH*. Goddammit, where is that fool girl?"

"Haven't seen her all day."

Lidah closed the pantry door and pressed her back against it. "Coming, Unc," she said. She clasped her shaking hands behind her.

At least he didn't look at her when she came in the room. Uncle Nolan did, and she ignored how red and raw his cheeks were and the slimey snail-trail tracks of tears running down both.

"Clean up this mess, girl," Uncle Bart said. "And I'll start our dinner."

The room was in disarray: furniture overturned and liquor spilled across the floor and Uncle Nolan had missed his bucket when he puked. She struggled not to wrinkle her nose and started by moving the chairs and the little low table away from the mess.

She had rinsed away the bile-and-whiskey puddles on the floor and was getting to scrubbing when she heard Uncle Bart call her again. Soft this time. Too soft.

She came into the kitchen and he was standing in front of the open pantry. Not knowing what it was doing—how could it—the clockwork cat was winding around Bart's ankles and the mismatched winding box stood clear out, it seemed, from the rest of its lithe body. "What's this," Uncle Bart said in that too-quiet voice.

"I found it," Lidah said. Her voice small. Mouse-like.

"*Found* it," he repeated. "Found it where, girl?"

"What's this here?" Uncle Nolan was saying behind them, the three of them crowded into the small kitchen. "When's dinner —?" Then he was looking down at the cat. "Huh. Looks just like that other one."

Bart wheeled on him. "What other one?"

Oh, if he just moved a little to the right, she could snatch up her things, she could go, right out the back kitchen door.

"There was one out in the street," Nolan was saying. And damn, he had always had a good memory for a drunk, remembering insults and slights as easy as anything, even after a stupor. "I broke it up, just for fun, y'know."

"Just to be cruel, you mean," Lidah said, even though she knew it would give her away. "Just because you're broke down and small and you want every lovely thing in the world to be broke down and small, too."

They stared at her, the two uncles, her mama's kind brothers.

Bart struck her—hard—across the face.

Nolan kicked the cat from where it was winding between his feet and Bart's. It clipped the wood and earthen wall, sending a shower of dust down around it, but it was unbroken. *"No!"* Lidah shrieked.

A horrible smile spread across Nolan's face; his eyes shone. "Don't like that, huh?" he said. He drew one of his pistols and pointed it at the cat. "How about this? Make it so you can't fix it up again, will I?"

"Don't," she begged. Still, he fired, of course he did, but he missed.

The cat was running. But it hadn't run before. Hadn't had a sense of self-preservation. Had only been a fragile toy, easily broken. Unresisting. But now it scampered out of the house like a real cat, like a magicked thing.

Oh, tinker-witch, Lidah thought, half in thanks and half in prayer. Nolan fired again out the kitchen door; the bullet winged into the dark. "*Stop* that," Bart ordered and grabbed for the weapon. Her uncles tussled there in the small kitchen, grunting. They lurched against the pantry door, which splintered, and into the cupboards and finally into the little stove with its coal belly and this they overturned, scattering its glowing contents across the floor.

Neither of them noticed this much because Nolan had his second pistol pointed at Bart's face. "Always pushing me around," he said. "Even when we were kids."

The floor was beginning to smoke. And the woven circle rug she'd made for the threshold. Lidah scrambled to the pantry and snatched up her little bag of things. Neither of the uncles was looking at her now. Bart had his hands raised in supplication. "Easy, huh, Nolan? Let's not be rash."

"Making me feel less than. Small," Nolan hissed. "Broken down, like she said."

"I'm sorry," Bart was saying, and the floor was beginning to crackle.

Lidah ran out the door, not stopping even at the crack of a gunshot.

She walked down the road out of town in the bluing twilight and after that she followed the moon's yellow smirk, creeping above the horizon. The clockwork cat scampered ahead of her. Its eyes glowed green in the dark. Every now and again, it mewed into the darkness, a crystal, chiming note. Lidah shifted her little sack of possessions onto her shoulder. Mama's quilt was folded in her arms. She'd need it, sooner than not.

Shadows had swallowed the dim watery lights of Mud Hollow when she heard the first thuds of hooves behind her. Wrong direction for settlers. A peddler maybe? Only if she was lucky. She scuttled off the path, and the cat followed.

A lantern bobbed down the road, as if disembodied, held aloft by some spirit heading home from its grim mission. But in reality, it was attached to a cart, and atop that cart sat the tinker-witch. "C'mon out, now," she said to the bushes.

Lidah obeyed and doing so saw that no ordinary beast pulled the tinker-witch's cart. It was a clockwork pony, thousands of clicking gears turning in perfect sequence as it trotted in place. She had never seen anything like it. Here and there she recognized pieces from the mine's automata, a gleaming mismatch of metal and parts.

"How?" she could only ask.

"Maybe I'll show you someday." The tinker-witch smiled. "Need a lift?"

Lidah scrambled up next to her on the cart's bench. She spread her mama's quilt across her lap. The clockwork cat, more gracefully, leaped onto the wheel and then settled between them. Its tail curled and uncurled. Its whiskers twitched.

"Penelope," the tinker-witch said and held out her hand.

Her palm was hard but smooth when they shook. "Lidah."

And the clockwork horse took them down the road into the evening: Lidah and the tinker-witch and the clockwork cat.

EAST WIND IN CARRALL STREET

HOLLY SCHOFIELD

Wong Shin pulled down on a lever, scraping his elbow against the metal framework within the clockwork lion. The lion obediently approached Margie where she stood in his family courtyard. Over and over, he made the lion step forward, then retreat, keeping a light hand on the crucial levers. When Margie shot a guilty look over her shoulder at the brothel behind her, Shin copied her glance, awkwardly peering upwards through the screening above the lion's broad nose. Margie's aunt was not at the second story window. He let out his breath. Fully four years older, he felt responsible that they not be seen together. Practice time was short so he gave all his attention back to the controls, completing the sequence of dance steps, as focused as if he were performing a traditional Chinese lion dance in front of his father's business associates rather than for the amusement of a ten-year-old White girl.

From his cramped spot behind the lion's eyes, he twisted a

bamboo rod, snapping the lion's mouth open and closed, imagining the traditional drum beats. As cables tightened, a pulley triggered another line attached to the puffy silk balls mounted on the lion's paper-mâché face. He let the silk decorations waggle a bit then he pressed a ceramic spring-loaded button next to his knees, sending the clockwork lion's gears ratcheting noisily. As he pumped his legs in the iron stirrups, the lion's front feet followed suit, dancing a complex jig. Dust billowed up between the gaps in the stirrups, making him cough.

He pranced again toward Margie, his knees reaching up around his ears. "Go away, Mah-jee, go away!" he called out, laughing.

Margie giggled and twirled out of his way. "You mean run away! Or flee!" she called back, eager to improve his English, as always.

He chased her across the unkempt courtyard, picturing the layers of colorful cotton swaying behind him. This morning's improvements meant the lion's iron framework was now the length of a large horse—fully a dozen *chek* long. There was nothing like the clockwork lion in the city of Vancouver's Chinatown, nor in British Columbia, nor perhaps in all of the Dominion of Canada—despite it being a complete sham.

Tomorrow, across Carrall Street at Teck Woo's new bakery, the drummers would play: at first, slow beats, then becoming gradually faster and faster. The crowds would yell encouragement and, as the excitement grew and the lion danced, Shin would snatch the all-important red envelope of money through the massive lion jaws. And no one would know that it wasn't a true clockwork lion.

Shadows crept up the brick wall of his father's grocery store as the afternoon wore on. A dial on the lion's interior panel indicated that the clockwork's energy coil was almost spent. Shin's arms and legs began to ache from the repeated motions in the confined space.

As he sashayed one more time across the yard toward Margie, making the ears wiggle and the beard shimmy, she looked past him toward the grocery and her eyes grew wide with fear. He stopped, in confusion, just as his father's voice rang out.

"Shin-Shin, neh jow mat yeh, wah? Shin-Shin, what are you doing?

Shin laboriously turned the lion fully around to face his father, hoping the cotton-clad framework would shield Margie's escape. She would need time to climb the fence and his father blocked the only front exit that led between brick buildings out to Carrall Street.

"Doy em jee, Baba." I'm sorry, Father.

"Why are you practicing out here? The neighbors must not see!" His father's village-accented Cantonese harshened in displeasure.

"Sorry, Baba, the workshop floor is not big enough anymore for the full routine." Shin let the lion's knees sag, relieved that Baba hadn't caught sight of Margie; his father was simply worried that the clockwork lion would be seen by the neighbors. No one in Chinatown, aside from Shin and his father, knew that the boy steered the lion from within. In the two years since the lion had been completed, Shin's father had convinced the Chinatown businessmen's association that the lion was truly clockwork-run. The scale and complexity of such clockwork had been attempted without success since the start of the Qing Dynasty and his father had quickly grown famous. If the businessmen knew that this lion was controlled by a boy pulling levers, they would not pay the ten-dollar fee for an opening good-fortune ceremony; instead they would hire Lee Chan and his brawny son to provide the two-dollar, man-powered version.

"Since you are already out here, practice the lettuce retrieval cere-mony. Grab that maple leaf up there." Shin's father pointed at the woodshed roof, cluttered with twigs and debris. "Balance your front legs on the old chicken coop."

"Yes, Baba." Shin steered the lion to the dilapidated wooden structure that hugged the woodshed. They hadn't had chickens since Mama had died during childbirth seven years ago. Now, thistles filled the coop, spilling out the top and sides through wire mesh. Shin pressed a lever to raise the lion's left foot onto the top corner of the rickety structure, praying to the earth god Dabo Gong that the chicken coop could withstand both the lion's and his weight. He knew he'd grown taller since Baba had designed the lion head when he was twelve—he was now up to Margie's shoulder—and he must have put on a few *catties* of weight too. He almost blurted out that this stunt would be more difficult than placing the lion's front legs on two pre-positioned barrels as he would tomorrow, but he bit the words back. Baba would know all that and have factored the risk, like men did. If it was fated to collapse, it would. Shin clamped his mouth shut, even as the huge lion foot made the top board creak. If he didn't attempt difficult things, Baba would never call him Ah Shin and treat him like the adult he was.

He eased his weight forward, the energy coil unwinding with a squeal. An indicator on the left panel said he had about ten *fan* of energy left—just enough to make the lion grab the large green leaf and drop down to kneel in front of Baba.

The chicken coop creaked again. Thistles rustled. Shin looked down between his leg stirrups. A wisp of blonde hair was caught among the thistles. More rustling and blue eyes peered up at him.

"Hurry up!" Baba's voice came from behind, near the grocery's rear door. His father must have stepped back, most likely expecting Shin to fail and fall. He hadn't seen Margie.

In the chicken coop, Margie's eyes filled with tears. The lion weighed as much as three men. If the chicken coop couldn't support its weight, it would surely crush her just as being born had crushed his little sister. The baby that was to be Shin's little sister had only lived a few days, not long enough to name.

Should he tell Baba that Margie was in the coop and save her life? She could run home. He glanced upward at the building behind. A woman with a mound of hair on her head stood at the brothel window, scanning the alleyway. His father would thrash him with a bamboo stick if he knew about Shin's friendship with Margie, but that was nothing compared to the beating Margie's aunt would give her for associating with filthy heathens such as himself.

Perhaps he could pretend to roll to one side, as if he wasn't in control? Surely the lion, made with his father's sturdy workmanship, could handle such a fall? But Shin would bring shame to his ancestors if the controls got smashed and were unable to function for tomorrow's ceremony.

Shin balanced on the left leg for so long, his thigh muscle trembled.

He heard his father hawk and spit on the ground in disgust at Shin's delay.

He couldn't crush Margie, he couldn't. Perhaps he could fall to the left, very slowly and gently, controlling the lion's iron spine. He raised the lion's right foot and placed it close, deliberately too close, to the left foot. He slowly eased the main lever upwards, arching the lion's spine, placing the centre of gravity slightly over the paws. Too much! The lion over-balanced and crashed forward. Shin quickly threw his body leftward. His head hit iron bars and the lion hit the ground. He closed his eyes until the dozens of sewn-on bells stopped jingling.

It was almost a relief when Baba, still swearing, opened the neck hinges so he could scramble out onto the dirt of the courtyard. The left side of the chicken coop was smashed to bits, loose boards dangling at all angles. Snapped cables littered the ground near the lion. The giant head was crushed and broken in several places. The far end of the chicken coop appeared undamaged but it was hard to tell.

He listened for the rustle of thistles as he helped Baba carry the broken pieces into the grocery-cum-workshop but heard only the inauspicious caw of a crow. He gave a final look back, the lion's bright horsehair tail dragging in the dust behind him, but there was nothing to be seen.

After a meal of rice and dried salmon, accompanied by unsellable black-edged greens, Shin crouched on the floor of the workroom. The lion head lay on a workbench and his father hunched over it, cursing loudly and slamming various hand tools around. The bakery opening would happen at first light. The almanac had been consulted and it was an auspicious day. The ceremony could not be delayed.

Shin's offers to help were ignored so he did his evening shop chores, including winding the springs on the little shop heaters needed to ward off the springtime chill. Shin's failure to do his duty to the family drummed through his head even as he took pride that his fingers no longer bled during the endless turning of the tiny keys. Small gadgets like the heaters could be human-wound, unlike larger coils that required teams of men trotting in circles, or oxen like the White Men used. The lion's clockworks were powered by a mid-sized coil and Baba had arranged delivery of a new pre-wound one at sunrise. The fee—a fifty-cent coin —gleamed under the oil lantern by the door.

Shin tinkered for a while with a clockwork monkey he had been working on for Margie. Over a period of months, he had taken apart an old tofu-maker and reassembled the sprockets and gears. He had shaped the framework from cedar, rather than the more traditional, and more expensive, bamboo. Daringly, he had travelled six blocks, his first foray outside Chinatown, giving his Spring Festival money to a dark-skinned Indian down by the stockade in exchange for a raw beaver pelt. After soaking the skin in an oak stump, he had softened it to a felt-like material that he thought might resemble monkey fur. He had crafted robes and a headband from scraps of Mama's dress that Baba had been using as a window covering. The shade of yellow matched the cover of Shin's proudest possession, a book of tales about the Monkey King's many journeys.

The rebuilt clockwork mechanism functioned well enough to make the monkey wave its hand; however, Shin wanted to do better. He took a used wax cylinder—its grooves blurred by overuse —and began to cut new and intricate lines with his pocketknife.

The day that Margie had shown him the White Men's wax cylinders had changed his life. She had snuck him into the whorehouse's laundry room to show him the shoe-polishing machine, thinking he would be impressed. Shin had opened the machine's repair hatch and been appalled at the White Man's crude and clumsy clockworks. "Like a beast would expel," he had told her. But, he had been fascinated with what had conveyed the wondrously precise instructions to the poorly engineered clockworks: wax cylinders, each grooved with a thousand tiny lines. Even the richest Chinese didn't have such marvels. When Margie had given him dozens of spent cylinders, he had clapped his hands in glee.

He put down the knife and opened a page in his second proudest possession, a programming manual that Margie had stolen for him last month. He had been explaining to her that the last new moon was the beginning of the Year of the Monkey and, later that day, she had brought him a slice of bread dripping with salt pork fat. She had some concept of birthing day anniversary gifts that made no sense to him. He had politely eaten the bread. Baba had told him many times that the diseases White Men got by drinking unboiled water and eating uncooked greens were many and complex, challenging even for Chinatown doctors and pharmacists. Shin had carefully watched his bowels for days but there appeared to be no ill effect from the treat.

He flipped a page in the book, looking for a certain coding sequence that would help the monkey move its tail in synchronization with its hands. Margie's aunt had boxed her ears soundly for the book theft but then covered for her, telling the irate customer it had been taken by one of the maids. Margie had spent hours teaching English numbers and coding symbols to Shin, as well as all the algebra and geometry she learned in the school for White children. In return, he had patiently drawn diagrams of simple clockworks on scraps of butcher paper, explaining them in his broken English, sitting cross-legged beside her in their favorite spot atop the greengrocery roof.

He tossed the monkey aside, not in the mood to work on it when all of his dreams were being dashed by his foolish actions. He watched Baba grapple with the broken lion as fresh waves of shame washed over him. Over the past few months, the yin and yang synergy of elegant Chinese clockworks and White Men's wax cylinders had filled his thoughts. Ideas had poured out of him faster than he could form the English words to tell Margie: how wax cylinders could perhaps someday be used to guide abacus beads, making giant calculating machines. When he was old enough to run Baba's greengrocery, he would investigate such things in the evenings, like men did, much as Baba tinkered nowadays with clockworks.

"Come." Baba pointed at the bicycle in the corner. Shin squeezed between crates of carrots and gear parts and mounted the bike. The length from the seat to the pedals had become too short for him. With a strong push, he started the pedals turning, then settled into a fast, even pace. In front of him, the lengthy bike chain spun and the friction welder started up. His father grasped an iron rod with bamboo tongs and pressed it in the collar of the welder. He touched the lower end of the rod to an interior brace of the lion head which lay wedged in a vise below.

As Shin kept up a furious pace, the rod began turning fast enough to blur. It would take a long while to heat enough to form a proper weld. He let his thoughts drift. There was no point in buying Margie *bao* or other pastries for her birth celebration, whenever it might occur; her calendar was too strange to have much meaning. Plus, she had smilingly refused every piece of food he had ever offered her. The thought of food made his stomach growl, empty again. As acrid smoke swirled around him, he imagined the wonderful contents of Teck Woo's market cart, soon to be a full-fledged bakery in a new finely-styled brick building across the street. Businesses were springing up every day. White Men might refuse to hire Chinese for even the worst jobs at Roger's Sugar Mill, but that would not break the businessmen's spirits; the community would build their own new China here in the Dominion of Canada.

"Steady, Shin-Shin," Baba said, as the end of the rod began to glow a cheery red. By the time the sun had set and the automated oil lanterns clicked on, the many necessary welds were completed. Shin stepped down and dried his sweat on his too-short jacket sleeve. His stomach rumbled again. The store's income was not enough to live on; without the lion ceremony earnings they would be hungry next winter, like they had been before Baba had built the wonderful mechanism.

Coming to the 'golden mountain' was to be a new start for the Wong family. Baba had come first, earning money laboring in the fields on the mainland to the east, paying off his head tax and landing fees. Years later, Mama had left her small village and travelled in what she had called 'in fear and boredom' along with several other women in a large stinking ship. Both had worked hard at the greengrocer business as baby Shin played on the store's splintery wood floor amid clucking chickens and broccoli stems. His first toy had been a broken abacus. His second was a broken automated wok-stirrer he had first turned into a toy warrior, then a stick-like doll for Margie.

Margie's story was similar. Her mother had come from a mountainous place over the ocean to the east, where people slid on snow with boards tied on their feet. Margie wanted to be an architect, designing buildings like the new brick Driard Hotel where fine ladies drank tea. Meanwhile, she did kitchen duty at the brothel, saving up customers tips for an architecture mail order course from the Simpsons catalogue. Once she had shown Shin a paint set a customer had given her. She had swirled powders together, yellow and blue. "That's like you and me, together we can make the Dominion of Canada better than either of the two alone." Shin had answered in his stumbling English that Canada was more like the many colors of vegetable fried noodles—a mixture of everything but a blend of nothing.

"Come. Try this." Baba's wiry body swung the lion head to the floor, not bothering with the hoist. Together they reattached the long body to the head in the cramped space, laying the drooping middle over some barrel staves at the rear of the shop and looping the legs and back feet towards the head by the big door at the front.

Shin swung his short queue over his shoulder to his front as he examined the rebuilt lion. It would be a tight fit. Baba had reinforced the head with more cross supports, threading iron rods past the leg braces to the back of the head. Shin hastily reattached the yellow cloth, sponging off the dirt from the yard, and brushing out the red and gold horsehair fringes while his father repositioned cable housings every which way. Baba was a competent craftsman, Shin suddenly realized, but his designs were less elegant than the sturdy oxen White Men used to wind coils.

"You, East Wind, get in." His father gave an impatient gesture and Shin got down on his knees beside the head, a second insight flooding into his head. His father's continual reference to the famous battle in China that depended on a late-arriving east wind—a wind crucial to the success of the fire ships being sailed toward the enemy—was not a compliment to Shin. Instead, his father was ashamed of their deception to the community and ashamed of the necessity of using Shin to operate the lion. Shin studied the stern line of his father's mouth. There was no time to dwell on the matter.

Shin bent his head so that Baba could lift the lion head over him. Bowing his head had not been necessary even three months ago. He must have grown a full *tsun*—a handsbreadth—since then. His wrists jutted out from his jacket as he helped lower the lion head over his own.

A gasp, a grunt, and the head—now probably weighing as much as Baba himself—came down hard on his thighs, cutting off all light but for a faint glow though the nose screen. One of the new iron rods crushed down on Shin's knees. He shoved a leg out the side of the head and under the huge rear paw on the side away from his father. He tucked his other foot under his buttocks, where it was useless to power the leg controls.

"Good, it works." In relief, Baba waggled one of the lion's silk balls, the connected bamboo handle striking Shin on the ear. "Now, get out. A short sleep is still possible."

Shin quickly tried various other positions as he clambered out from beneath, Baba holding the lion head aloft. In the poor light, Baba hadn't noticed Shin's struggles, how his legs stuck out. How he had failed.

Shin's mouth tasted like raw bitter melon.

He no longer fit inside the lion.

A small part of him thrilled at the thought that Baba's shameful fraud could not continue. He pushed the thought away. The red envelope money would go unearned. He had let down Baba and all Wong ancestors. And Teck Woo's bakery would forever have bad luck.

As his father climbed the narrow stairs heading to the sleeping mats, Shin stayed huddled on the cold dirt floor. He didn't deserve to sleep tonight.

The lion weaved and dodged, as graceful as bamboo in the wind. It danced closer to the barrels, surrounded by smiling, dark jacketed men who nodded with delight. Lucky green onions tied to its horns waved merrily. The drummers intensified the beat, luring the lion closer and closer to the leafy green lettuce hanging over the bakery doorstep and the red envelope tied within. The lion approached, cocked its head at the lettuce, put a foot on a barrel, then stepped off again, turning its head to wink coquettishly at the crowd.

A toddler emerged from between a man's legs and headed for the lion, probably attracted by the glittering metal discs sewn to the red and yellow layers of cloth. The lion continued to dance, oblivious, stepping forward and back in a tradition as old as gunpowder.

From his perch atop the greengrocery roof, Shin wrapped his arms around his bruised knees, the clay tiles cold under his thin slippers.

Finally, a woman scuttled from between the men and grabbed the child's arm, dragging it back into the crowd.

Shin let out his breath. The monkey's cylinder programming was set to a specific pattern. There was no altering it, for toddlers or anything else. He pictured the energy coil unwinding in the body of the lion, powering the mechanism even as the monkey pushed and pulled levers and switches in an intricate pattern; its hands and feet, even its tail, manipulating the lion in a dance more complex than a Chinese acrobatic display, all seven cylinders spinning madly. With wooden blocks tied to its feet and a wire hook embedded in its tail, the monkey had fit inside the lion perfectly. He had used the yellow robes to tie it securely to the framework.

"That's charming, that is." Margie settled beside him on the roof, tucking her green skirts immodestly under her. Her right arm hung in a sling made from a paisley scarf and a long scratch ran down one cheek.

"Therefore no birth present for you," Shin answered tensely, keeping his eyes on the lion.

Margie giggled. "I never understand you even when I understand you. Here, I brought you a present because you saved me. Don't worry—I waited until dark yesterday then I told my aunt I fell from a tree." She shoved a pastry in his hand, ruby and gold in the morning sun. "It's called rhubarb pie."

"Rhu-bah pie," Shin repeated absently and bit into it. He hadn't had time for rice porridge this morning and working hard all night had made his stomach hollow. Baked wheat flour and tart juice filled his mouth, sliding down as pleasantly as Teck Woo's sweet red bean *jian dui.*

The clockwork lion grabbed the lettuce in the final dance sequence, as the drumbeats grew staccato. From his vantage point above, Shin saw the small brown hand flash out and draw the red envelope inside the jaws. The crowd cheered, Baba loudest of all. For the first time since he'd seen Margie hiding in the chicken coop, Shin began to relax.

Finished, the lion lumbered back across the street, the crowd parting way. A grinding noise drifted up as the grocery's large workroom door opened, its escapement mechanism perfectly timed. The lion marched steadily toward the grocery as the door rose higher and higher. Several *chek* before the workroom entrance, the lion turned sharply to the right, stepped up onto the wooden sidewalk and rammed face-first into the grocery's brick wall.

"Ah Shin! Ah Shin!" Baba rushed toward the lion as it made a horrid grinding noise and the front legs collapsed.

On the roof above, Shin bit down on his knuckles. Baba's use of 'Ah Shin'—the adult form of his name—shone through the awfulness of the crash.

Below, his father prodded the ruins of the lion. He gave a start then, just before the other men reached him, pulled off the yellow restraints and shoved the monkey beneath his jacket. He made calming gestures at the men and laughed with an open mouth. His words drifted upwards —assurances that the lion could be repaired. After all, he said, it was clockwork run and the best technology in all the continents.

Shin licked blood off his knuckles, careful of the large blister on his hand—a result of winding the monkey's coil for many *fan* last night. He felt his chest swell with pride. Combining the White Man's cylinder tech-nology with traditional clockwork meant that the shameful deception of the lion could stop. And, equally importantly, his father saw him as a man.

He looked out over the rooftops as a gentle rain started. In the distance, Chinatown's clay tiles blurred together with the White Man's cedar shingles.

He grinned at Margie and crammed the rest of the pastry in his mouth. "Two countries, both East Wind," he said around oily crumbs and laughed when she shook her head in confusion.

DEM BONES
ANNE STOLINSKY

"Careful with that coffin, boy. It has my son in it."

"Yes, Ma'am." The porter returned to his task. The box was small, its dimensions no more than two feet by two feet, and feather-light, its warm honey-brown sides and bottom patched to prevent the ashes within from spilling out. The porter, a superstitious man, handled the coffin carefully, but sped through boarding the train, wanting to be done with his task of placing it in her train compartment.

The elderly woman paused to place a stray gray hair back into its bun. Her wrinkled hands, speckled with prominent age spots, pulled her shawl closer around her shoulders. Her patched dress, once as brilliantly yellow as sunshine, was faded and threadbare from years of wear. With difficulty, she reached her withered hands to the railing to steady herself while boarding, but then her foot slipped off the top step. Falling forward, leaning backward, trying to recapture her balance, she felt a hand on her shoulder. A man, dressed in the familiar blue of a Union soldier, steadied her so she could continue her climb.

"Thank you, Sir." She gasped as her free hand moved to her mouth. She whispered, "You look like him." Leaning against the doorframe, she began, "My son, my Elijah, served at Gettysburg. Were you there?"

"Ma'am, no, I wasn't." He tipped his hat. "Mayhap we will meet again on board."

The porter looked behind him to ensure she was following down the aisle of the wood-paneled train car. The woman's shoes made scratching sounds on the bare floor. She reached the compartment just after the porter. The porter juggled the coffin to allow better access to the handle. Her body stiffened. Her hand reached for the handle to the compartment as quickly as a viper's attack, and opened it before the porter could.

"Thank you, Ma'am, for the assistance," the porter mumbled.

"You're not gonna lose my son's remains for me, not after the long trek I've taken," she retorted.

The porter motioned for her to enter. The compartment looked comfortable, with two bench seats upholstered in cream-colored fabric with small golden buttons. Cream-colored curtains with tassels adorned the room's two windows. A door on the wall above each bench opened to a small storage area.

"Want me to put this box in the storage, Mrs. Settler?"

"No, thank you. I'll keep my boy with me. Put him on the seat."

The porter carefully placed the coffin on the seat, bowed, and left. She sat on the bench opposite the coffin, dropping her hat and purse next to her.

She gazed out the window for a few minutes, needing a respite. She reached into her purse, removing a bud from a lavender plant she had harvested before leaving home. The fragrant scent of the rest of the buds in her purse filled the compartment.

She smiled, her thoughts returning to the day she harvested

the plants, the day before she left on this journey to reclaim Elijah's ashes. She had walked around the side of her house. Sunrise reflected in the windows elicited a gasp from Johanna at the beauty. She marveled at how well her plants looked. Striding up and down the rows, she selected a bud of this, a twig of that. When her basket was full, she turned away from the garden and walked into the barn.

She had placed the wicker basket carefully on the floor. She cleared the top of a table of its contents, moving horse feed and small spades. She placed butcher paper on the cleared table top, then began to pull twigs and buds out of the basket. The bud of one plant went to the top of the paper, a twig of another at the bottom. Each herb was placed in a specific order, none on top of the other, as few as possible touching the others. *The herbs will dry by the time I get home with Elijah.*

The train lurched, and she reached over to carefully place the coffin on her lap. Cradling it in her arms, she sobbed, something she had not allowed herself to do since hearing of Elijah's death. She hadn't even cried in front of the soldiers who gave her his ashes. "We're sorry for your loss Mrs. Settler. But be proud of your boy. Elijah, he died fighting, killed him five Johnny Rebs before he went down." The soldier's voice lowered slightly. "A fire broke out right next to our position, Ma'am. There ain't a lot left of him, but we gathered as much as we could." He hesitated, then spoke again. "Elijah spoke of you, telling us how much he loved his Ma." Eyes down, the soldier shuffled from one foot to the other. "Here, Ma'am. Here's Elijah's remains."

She took the box from the soldier, bravely standing as straight as she could. She thanked them for bringing the coffin to her at the train station.

The train ride from Revere, Massachusetts, to Gettysburg, Pennsylvania, was a long one, filled with anticipation. Now that she was on her way back home to Revere, she felt the loss of her son more poignantly.

"I'm gonna take you home, Elijah. Home's where you belong. Your friend Perry is taking care of the farm while I'm gone. He misses you too."

An overwhelming exhaustion filled her. She placed the coffin on the floor and curled up next to it. With her hand touching the warm wood, she slept.

"Thank you for picking me up at the train station, Perry." Johanna Settler waved the teenaged son of her neighbor toward the table in the kitchen, indicating without words for him to place the coffin there. The coffin, while small, took up most of the table top. The honey-brown wood contrasted with the table's deep cherry color. Two chairs of the same cherry wood were pushed away from the table.

"You're welcome, Mrs. Settler. I'm gonna miss Elijah too. Pa said to tell you to let him know if you need anything." Perry walked to the door to leave. His hand on the knob, he turned back toward Johanna. "Are they sure that's Elijah in that box? The soldiers were sure he's dead?" Mrs. Settler nodded, grateful for his concern. "I know you two were close, but yes, that's my boy in there." The teenager sniffed, holding back a sob, then left.

Johanna sat, hands folded on her lap, thankful for the peace and quiet. Her journey to and from Gettysburg had been the most arduous trip of her life. Tears threatened to stream down her face. She clenched her jaw. "Not gonna cry again. Not today. Not any day." Holding her head high, she walked to her bedroom.

Sunlight warming her eyelashes woke Johanna the next morning. Shaking her body awake, she marveled that she slept. *Having Elijah home again is good for me.*

The chickens screamed as she strode to the coop. She reached in and grabbed one, ignoring the blood dripping from her hand as it pecked at her. She placed the screaming chicken into a small cage, leaving it near the coop.

She walked to the stable next. Brushing the chestnut-colored horses brought tears to her eyes. This had been Elijah's task. He loved the horses as much as he loved his Ma.

Satisfied her horses looked healthy and that her neighbors took good care of her farm while she was away, she hitched the horses to the buggy, picked up the chicken in the cage, and rode off.

The familiar dusty road gave her a sense of comfort after the long journey through unfamiliar ground. Her shoulders relaxed, and she smiled. Unraveling her bun, she laughed as the breeze blew her hair in front of her face, forming gray waves. She stopped at her neighbor's farm to give them a thank-you present of the chicken, before going into town for supplies.

A sharp yelp greeted her as she brought her supplies into the kitchen.

"Watch it, dog. If you don't want to be stepped on, then don't get under my feet."

She put the wicker basket on the table in the dining area. The farm was a good size, about thirty acres, but the house was small. Still, she reflected, it was good enough for her and her husband, God rest his soul, to have loved and lost each other. He died when Elijah was just a babe. It was a good enough size for her to have raised her son on her own, without having to depend on anyone. *Elijah was a good boy, helped his Ma whenever I asked. And even when I didn't ask, he took it on hisself to do.* Tears formed, but did not fall.

Her footsteps sounded loudly on the wood floor as she carried a few of the items from the basket into the kitchen. Johanna bent down to place her cheek against the coffin. "Tomorrow's the day Elijah. Be patient. We'll get you buried tomorrow. Your Ma promises."

The next morning, Johanna awoke before the rooster, to a dark sky. She paused to put on a light shawl before going outside. Standing near the house, she surveyed her land. *Can't bury him over here, not next to the garden.* Turning from north to east, south to west, her vision was filled with hay, golden stalks waving in the light breeze. A small area close to the barn was bare. *That's where I'll bury my son, near the barn with the horses he loved, and the hay he'd put in his mouth and chew while working.*

Her shovel kicked up a fine spray of silt as it struck into the dirt. Plunging the shovel in again and again, she dug a hole big enough to hold the coffin. Small pebbles of powdery soil rolled down the pile that grew next to the hole with each plunge. She stopped digging to wipe the sweat from her forehead. Silt mixed with sweat formed a muddy line across her brow. She coughed, unable to get the taste of the silt and mud out of her mouth. Johanna dug again, making the hole larger than the box she would be placing in its depths. "Gotta give it some room to grow," she muttered to herself. Finally satisfied with the size of the grave, she returned to the house. Washing her hands in the kitchen sink, she looked at the box on the table. "Don't want to dirty your coffin, Son."

She took the butcher paper she bought at the store and went outside to the grave again. The sun was just rising, presenting her with a sky filled with blues, pinks, and oranges. Johanna took this beauty as a positive sign from above. She said a silent prayer of thanks, then returned to her task.

Bending, she lost her balance and ended up sitting on the dusty ground. Turning to kneel, she carefully placed the butcher paper into the hole. She smoothed out the brown paper, leaving no creases, ensuring the entire floor of the tomb was covered. She stared at the sides of the grave. *Don't think I need to cover the sides too.*

Johanna grabbed the shovel, then planted the scoop end in the dirt. Her hands slowly moved up the handle, her body and feet moving with the upward progress. She'd done more work today than normal, and it was still early. Her feet ached, her hands, even though calloused, were sore and bleeding. She kept focused on her task, unwilling to allow the frailties of her body to sway her from burying her son. Her back threatened to cripple her as she walked to the barn.

She squatted down in front of the herb-covered table. Her

fingers blindly searched for a latch under the table. She found the latch and pushed. A hidden drawer opened slowly, groaning as it slid. Johanna made a mental note to oil the drawer next chance she got. She removed a small ceramic mortar and pestle from its resting place at the back of the drawer.

She began to stand, then lost her balance again when a stabbing pain shot through her back. The table tottered as she bumped against it. Wrinkled hands reached out to steady the table before her precious herbs could fall. She crawled to the wall of the barn, using it to help her upright.

The chickens and the rest of the farm were up and making noise. Johanna's attention was fixed on her task, ignoring the caws and clucks and moos. The animals would wait. She had more important things to attend to right now.

Gnarled fingers picked up the mortar and pestle. She sniffed the pestle. The pungent smell brought back memories of the last time it was used.

Johanna and her husband Aaron tried for years to have children, with no success. They were both growing older. Johanna's desire to bear a child was too strong for her to deny. Using some of her herbs, and this mortar and pestle, she prepared a mixture that she placed into her body, in the place that only her husband had ever touched. Within days she was pregnant with Elijah. Her husband was ecstatic, praising God for her pregnancy. Johanna knew the truth. She never shared her secret with Aaron. He wouldn't have understood.

Johanna and Aaron lived in Revere, Massachusetts, about an equal distance from Boston and Salem. Even though two centuries had passed since the fears of Salem, people still had a distrust of things they didn't understand. Had he known her secrets, Aaron may have declared her a witch.

Johanna carefully picked up one of the dried buds. Bits of the buds and twigs fell from her fingers as she twisted each, one by one. Reds, greens, purples, browns, the colors of the plants gave the mixture a brilliant rainbow effect. Johanna ground each bit until the mortar contained nothing but a fine powder. Each plant grain retained its color. The powder's colors were still as brilliant as when the bits were on the plants. Her fingers, hurt and bloody from digging, now felt light as she lovingly mixed the powder.

Johanna covered the mortar with a small piece of butcher paper and carried it to Elijah's grave. She stood straight and tall, the memory of the pains of her body erased. Holding the mortar in both hands, she lifted it toward the blue, cloudless sky. A tune came unbidden from her lips, with words that had been passed down in her family from generation to generation. Her face tilted toward the sun, her eyes shone. Her song finished, she placed the mortar on the ground, then gathered her dress about her and knelt. She dipped her fingers into the vessel and sprinkled the mortar's contents into the freshly dug grave. When she was finished, no sign of the paper remained. It was covered with fine powder.

Though exhausted, she felt like skipping as she made her way to the kitchen. She carefully picked up the coffin and carried it lovingly to the grave. The box fit in the hole perfectly. Picking up the shovel, she refilled the hole. She poured water onto the grave, singing to it, "Slumber on Baby Dear," a tune she had sung many times to her son as a baby.

Johanna watered the site every day before starting her chores. After a few days, sprouts appeared, their green shoots poking up from the middle of the plot. Each day she watered and watched the sprouts grow.

Three weeks later Johanna awoke, grabbed the watering can, then walked outside to water the sprouts. To her delight, the sprouts had formed into a sapling. She danced around the newly formed young tree, humming.

After two months, the tree was fully grown. Johanna marveled at the strong limbs and stout trunk. The tree stood five feet tall, with branches spreading out about ten feet wide. The leaves, a wondrous sight of reds, greens, purples, and browns, dazzled in the sunshine. Each day Johanna continued to water the tree, singing as she worked.

She plucked the first growth from the tree with little problem. It was on the bottom branch, within her outstretched arm's reach. She twisted the green leaf that held the growth on the tree, releasing the small bone into her hand. *Probably belongs to his hand or foot.* The woman danced again, danced and sang the songs of her ancestors. She placed the bone into a small box in the barn, similar in size to the coffin buried underneath the tree. "First one, first one. Not the last one!" she sang aloud.

Weeks later, Johanna brought a ladder out to the tree from the barn. She needed assistance to reach the branch closest to the top. The ladder tottered as Johanna's arm stretched as far as it could. Her fingertips lightly brushed the branch, but couldn't get a firm grasp. She clambered down the ladder, moved it a few feet to the left, and remounted. *Better.* Holding the branch carefully with her left hand, she used her right to pluck the skull from the purple leaf. Johanna sighed as she climbed down, a contented yet anxious sigh. She peered into the sockets where the eyes should have been. *Soon will be again.* With one finger, she traced the curves of the eye sockets, the jaw bone, the nose... Harvesting the skull rendered the tree bare. *The next step will begin tomorrow.*

Bones lined the floor of the barn like a gigantic jigsaw puzzle. Johanna frowned as she realized she had placed the leg bones where the arm bones should be. Removing them required grace and a light step. Finally satisfied the skeleton was accurate, she stepped back. *Only a few more tasks to complete.*

Johanna returned to the house, lifted her rifle, and checked to make sure it was loaded. Back in the barn, she aimed the sight on the left shin bone. The rifle recoiled as she shot one bullet into the skeleton. Bone fragments sprayed away from the semi-shattered leg. *I'm sorry Elijah. But I had to do it this way. I'll be tellin' folks you were found in a hospital with a leg shattered, not dead. It's the only way to explain how you came back.*

She hurried to make final preparations. Her fingers again found the latch under the table, releasing the hidden drawer. Reds, greens, purples, browns, still filled the mortar. Johanna sprinkled the remaining fine powder over the skeleton. Bits of color rained down on the stark white bones spread out on the barn floor. The mortar emptied, Johanna scrutinized the skeleton before her, ensuring all was covered. Smiling, she sang, all the songs of her youth, the songs she sang to Elijah when he was young, the songs of her ancestors, all the songs of her soul. She sang until the sun began its trek downward. She sang until exhausted, when she lay down and slept.

She awoke with the rising sun. Next to her slept Elijah. Johanna's heart overflowed with love. *Only a mother can love this much.* Her son lay naked, his left leg scarred, showing evidence of a healed bullet wound. Her fingers tentatively reached out to touch this miracle, but she withdrew them before she made contact. She wanted him to sleep, not to wake up until she was ready. Johanna ran to the house to get clothes for her son. "My boy is home," she sang. "My son is home."

The Stolen Child

Gavin Bradley

Under the bright summer moon, she saw them dance.
They had not been there the night before; only appeared
when long shadows gave way to silver in the short, dark night.

Ethereal, laughing creatures visible through a gap
    in the field stone wall,
where moonlight and the other world poured through,
on the night when the dark was short lived, but full of magic.

She heard the voices call, high and sweet.
"Such a pretty child. Why not come and dance with us?"
She had heard the tales of travellers,
stories of *'other folk'* and children
snatched in the night, never to return.

But she was not afraid, could not be afraid,
of skin so fair in the moonlight,
of footfalls so soft as they twirled and spun
to the music, which beckoned her with every note,
punctuating the silence of the short, dark, summer night:
"Oh faerie child come out and play,
Under the brilliant moon of May,
No horseshoes here to trouble ye',
In silverlight, you'll dance with me."

A piercing blue eye appeared before her,
peering curiously out through the gap in the stone.
Then a kindly smile,
and a pale hand reached out, fingers curling in welcome.
She could not refuse such beauty,
and as the hole between worlds widened,
she crawled through to a world where
the music stopped.
The laughter became cackles and breathless whispers,
telling someone to "do it, do it *now!*"
Something struck her on the head, and from behind,
    and from the side;
She felt a rib crack.
She lay there, dizzy, before
slipping helplessly into
the short, dark summer night.

She awoke in an iron cage engulfed by pain,
    surrounded by laughter.
Not the pleasant trills of the dancing children,
she had yearned to join.
The laughter rode on foul-stenched breath

of tavern-dwelling men, who in their brutish humanity
shook the bars of dreaded iron,
bellowed and belched their great jokes.

Somewhere near the cage door,
a great fat man, rose-faced, roared and spat:
"See the faerie child! Captured, sneakin' 'cross the wall
to snatch our children from their beds!"
The faerie child, hugging her knees,
peered up from between
silver strands of hair;
her new window into the world of men.
They stared at her like pink rodents;
dirty and vulgar, upright and hairless.
Some children, the moonlight dancers,
surrounded the iron hutch and
threw rocks which cut and stung,
singing in ugly accompaniment:
"Oh faerie child come out and play,
Under the mother moon of May,
Kept under horseshoes you shall be,
In iron chains, you'll dance for me."

They left her shivering,
sticky with foul ale, cut by cruel stones.
In the iron prison, she cried.
She cried to her mother
who hung low in the summer night,
for the fair folk are people of The Moon;
daughters and sons of Elatha.
Her mother listened. Her mother heard.
The silver beams slithered into the tavern
through a high, open window,

and a ghostly tendril weaved its way towards her cage,
stopping at a thick, iron lock.
Click.

The faerie child looked up at the stream of silver,
winding its soundless way back out
through the small patch of night.
She pushed at the door,
wincing at the cold iron's burn.
It swung open with ease.

As she walked away from the cage,
and pushed through the tavern door
into the short, bright summer night,
illuminated by her smiling mother,
she felt the strength return to her bones;
an iron-like strength that humans could not know.
Basking in the bright moonlight,
in the once dark, summer night,
she looked down upon a sleeping village.
The stone-throwing, children would be asleep in their beds.
The fat, ale-drinking men, would be dreaming
     of cruel tricks and cages.
Her smile gleamed silver in the moonlight,
and as she strolled towards the village, she began to sing:
"Oh human child come out and play,
Under the mother moon of May,
No iron chains where we shall be:
Across the wall you'll dance for me..."

Pit Shop
Gary Buller

Brandon Wright had driven past the strange little pet shop more times than he cared to recall. He travelled that route at least once a week with his wife and daughter on their way to the megamarket to get their groceries. Now, stood outside the slightly ramshackle corner building with dirty windows and peeling woodwork, he intended on going inside for the first time. His feet seemed to have other ideas, though.

Brandon was ashamed to admit to himself that he felt a little uncomfortable. The truth was that he just didn't enjoy meeting new people. Even speaking to them on the telephone intimidated him a little. His wife, Sandra did all the talking when it came to ringing up the car insurance, or dealing with the teachers at Holly's school and it had always been that way as far back as he could remember. He just wasn't a 'people person' he supposed.

That was not the sole reason for Brandon's discomfort though, no, there was a creepy feeling to the old place. He had never once seen anyone come in or out of this establishment during the brief window in which he drove past, and that was a bit strange. Surely a pet shop sold animals, or at the very least pet supplies? Had a dull light not shone through the window or the sign been flipped to 'Open,' he would have thought it closed. Indefinitely.

The window display contained a large vivarium filled with the usual accessories lizard owners would be familiar with; water bowl, wood bark and a little cave at the front, plastic leaves at the back. In the middle of this a green lizard sat motionless. Brandon tapped the window, expecting to see its head move jerkily in response. It was only when it didn't move, and he saw painted blood dripping from its eyes that he realised it was plastic.

He recalled watching a documentary about these strange animals on the Discovery channel. These particular lizards squirted blood from their eyes as a defence mechanism, or so he seemed to remember. It was hard to imagine such a creature existed. To see a fake one sat there, staring at him with red streaked cheeks was just plain kooky. Brandon hesitated for a moment, looked at the strange window display and then back at his car before summoning the strength to push the door open. *Curiosity killed the cat,* he thought.

A bell tinkled as he stepped inside. A spring restrained the door and it closed slowly behind him. Immediately he picked up the sweet liquorice smell of cherry blend tobacco, sawdust and dry pet food. The smoke drifted around an elderly gentleman, who reclined behind a low counter top that had seen better days. He looked off into the middle distance in a way that only pipe smokers seem to do, his eyes misty and thoughtful under his flat cap.

It was silent for a couple of seconds, and Brandon was about to open his mouth when the man spoke. "Help you?"

"Um, yes," Brandon said. "I'm after some wax worms please, if you have them."

The old man rolled his eyes, exhaled and lifted himself from the rocking chair with exaggerated effort. "We're all out of the good ones," he said, "I put an order in 'couple of days ago now, and they still ain't delivered. Some of them are dead. I'll charge you half price if that's OK?"

"That's fine," Brandon replied.

The old man reached under the counter and pulled out a plastic tub containing dozens of the wiggling white creatures, at least half of them were black and didn't move.

"What critter you got?" the old man asked. He wore denim dungarees over a gingham shirt. It was an odd combination.

"Leopard Gecko, it's my daughter's."

"You like exotics then?"

"I suppose so. I didn't have much choice in the matter, honestly," he replied with a nervous chuckle.

The old man removed his pipe and looked Brandon in the eyes as if weighing him up. There was another uncomfortable silence before he spoke.

"You want to see something unusual?"

He nodded over his shoulder. Brandon looked past him and saw a doorway behind the counter leading to a dimly lit room. He could make out the glow of UV bulbs inside long, dark tanks, and the shimmer of light reflecting on glass surfaces.

Brandon weighed things up quickly, decided that the old fellow looked harmless enough and was intrigued to see what wonderful creatures lay just out of view. It later occurred to him that this was when things started to go wrong. His point of no return.

"Sure," he said, leaving the wax worms on the side.

The old man lifted a hinged corner of the counter and let him through.

Brandon crossed the threshold first, and was surprised at how dark and warm it was. There was a tropical heat and an odour of damp humidity. The UV lamps inside the vivaria were the sole source of light. The old man ushered him through into a small kitchen which smelled pungent and gamey. A hole had been cut into one corner of the ceiling where a chicken wire cage descended to the floor.

Brandon leaned against the sink unit, basin at his back. The old man flicked a switch on a kettle that looked too old to be powered by electricity. "Cuppa?" he asked, removing the pipe.

"No thanks."

"Please yourself."

"What exactly have you got that's so 'unusual' mister...?"

"Horace. Just call me Horace."

Brandon smiled, a local name if there ever was one. "I'm Brandon, by the way."

Horace didn't return the smile. "I've got lots of *unusual* things here Mister Brandon. Upstairs, for example, I have snakes that are illegal in this country because they're so venomous. I also have a few lizards that are on the endangered species register, but those are in my private quarters." He replaced the pipe and inhaled.

"Guess what lives in that cage?" he asked enigmatically, gesturing to the corner of the room.

Brandon craned his neck to peer into the pitch-black opening in the ceiling. Something large moved noisily in the roof space. He moved closer, the hairs on the back of his arms rising.

"Careful," Horace warned. "He'll have your fingers off."

Something large dropped from the void and landed with an agile *thump* on the hay strewn floor of the cage. It was a mass of matted grey fur and yellow teeth. Brown, vein streaked eyes glared at Brandon with wild malevolence. The creature launched itself at the wall of the cage with a furious screech. Brandon fell onto the tile floor, the chicken wire before him bowing under the weight of an animal bigger than his six-year-old daughter.

Horace chuckled as if he'd been told a particularly witty joke. "Momo, calm down." he said. "It's only a guest. This is Brandon."

The primate eyed him cautiously, before ascending a rope back into the ceiling space, moving with skittish agility. An odour of damp fur and faeces lingered.

Brandon climbed to his feet, heart thudding in his chest. He felt a little foolish and leaned back on the counter before facing the old man. "What the hell was that?" he asked, breathless.

"That was Momo, he's a..." Horace waved the thin end of his pipe in the air as he searched for the right word, "he's a *special* breed of ape. I got him from the same supplier that got me the crocodile."

"Crocodile?" Brandon asked. He didn't like where this conversation was going, nor the amusement on the old man's lips.

"Yes, the one behind you."

Brandon spun to face the basin. He hadn't noticed the eight-foot long tank sitting on the window sill above the sink. Lying within twelve inches of murky water, the golden-eyed reptile basked motionless under a heat lamp. It was almost as big as the tank itself. Through the disbelief and amazement, Brandon couldn't help but think how cruel it was keeping such a magnificent, and dangerous creature in those conditions.

"He's off to the zoo come July," Horace said, as if reading his thoughts. "He won't be with us long. My contact found him floating around Bottom's reservoir. He'd been living off ducks and geese, but chased a couple of lads out canoeing."

"Impossible," Brandon said. "It's too cold for reptiles in these parts."

Horace laughed again. This time, there was something distinctly condescending about his tone. "Cryptids," he said, simply.

"Pardon me?"

"Cryptids. Animals that shouldn't exist, but there's evidence they might. That's my speciality here Mister Brandon. I suppose technically speaking, they're not cryptids anymore because they *are* here and they *do* exist, I care for the bloody things after all— but I keep them a mystery so the world can keep wondering." He smiled at this, pulling out a packet of tobacco.

"You are joking, right?"

"What do you think Momo is?" Horace said, nodding again to the cage. "He was trapped in the woods of Louisiana, Missouri. You won't believe what I had to pay for him, but as far as I'm concerned, it's a bargain. Who else owns an ape-man? Of course, I'll have to buy a bigger cage because the adults grow to eight feet tall, he's only a nipper at the moment, but I don't mind. We have a bond."

Brandon shook his head, he couldn't believe it. *He must be stark raving mad,* he decided. "The crocodile isn't a cryptid, though. Is it?"

"The species isn't–but William is. Goodness knows how he came to stalk youngsters in the icy waters of Bottom's reservoir, but there he is–a regular mystery. As far as my collection goes he's unimpressive, hence why I asked the zoo to take him off my hands."

Brandon couldn't help himself. The logical part of his mind told him he'd seen an ape and a crocodile, not two mythical creatures. The curious little boy in him was intrigued, though and wanted to see more. "What else do you have?" he asked.

The old man pocketed his tobacco and led him out of the room, back into the eerie purple glow of the vivarium lined chamber. He stopped at an aquarium in one corner and gestured for his guest to look. At first, Brandon couldn't see anything in the water. There was a decorative skull lodged in the gravel and a thick row of gently waving sea grass at the rear. A photograph of a shipwreck served as an interesting backdrop.

"I almost forgot," Horace muttered. He opened a little draw underneath and removed an opaque container holding live pinkie mice. He took one, writhing between tobacco-stained finger and thumb, and dropped it into the water with a *plop*. Two unusually serpentine fish glided serenely from out of the hollow eyes of the skull. *Eels, perhaps?* Brandon suppressed a gasp.

One of them spun a slow motion pirouette in a stream of bubbles rising from the filtration tube and turned to face him. A gaunt, skeletal head with perfectly white eyes studied Brandon as it propelled itself with tiny webbed claws. Its upper body was colourless, tapering into a scaled tail that glowed green and purple under the UV lights. The tints reminded Brandon of an oil slick and he had a gut feeling that these little monsters were just as toxic. No money on earth would have persuaded him to put a single finger in that water.

"Mermaids," said Horace. "More common than you think, to be honest. They only grow to a foot long in captivity but have drowned many a sailor out at sea. These ones are from Lillesfjord in Norway, but I keep having to replace them every couple of years. They don't last long in these tanks."

One mermaid was slightly quicker and reached the pinkie mouse first. It opened and extended its jaws like a snake, taking a chunk out of the creature with rows of needle-sharp teeth. Blood billowed from the wound, clouding the water. When it cleared, the mermaids had retreated to the skull, gnawing the rodent's severed head. Floating just beyond the reach of light, they gazed out at Brandon with an interest he found very creepy.

"Vicious little buggers, aren't they?" Horace chuckled. He had moved to a tank on the other side of the room.

Brandon joined his host with perspiration beading his forehead. Crouching slightly, his face a couple of feet away from the glass, he observed an arboreal vivarium almost as tall as he was. Inside, two bare bulbs shone. He guessed this was to simulate sunlight and provide warmth. The bottom of the tank was lined with faux turf and dead leaves. A tree trunk extended from the bottom to the top of the enclosure.

Horace tapped gently on the glass. Three butterflies fluttered out of one of the hollows, landing on one of the branches criss-crossing the tank. Except they were not butterflies at all. Each one was a tiny, perfectly formed person with gossamer wings. Delicate veins spread through each wing, reminding Brandon of a stained-glass window. Their skin was mottled in pastel shades of green and brown, and they spoke to each other in a series of chatters and clicks.

"Beautiful," Brandon whispered. "So beautiful."

They flew from their branch to meet him, moving with a nimble gracefulness. He focused on their enchanting emerald eyes. So small, but so perfect. The room around him drifted away and the low hum of air pumps was in a different galaxy. He saw a minute pupil within a green eye, and it grew bigger and bigger until it swallowed him.

There was his father, a man who had died years before, larger than life. His belt strap, *Old Faithful,* rested in his palm.

"Drop your shorts and bend over, boy." He hissed at Brandon. "I'll teach you to disobey me! I told you to stay away from the old paper mill. Curiosity killed the cat, you know?"

Brandon obeyed—what more could he do? Rough, angry hands gripped him, bending him over a bony knee. The shadow of *Old Faithful* rose, buckle first, into the air. Then it fell with such velocity that a scream escaped him like bats from a crawlspace.

Brandon came to his senses. Horace had slapped him hard across the cheek, leaving a warm imprint. The tank front now had a small spiderweb of fractured glass. When he touched his forehead, there was blood on his fingers.

"Never get too close to the fairies," Horace said firmly, emphasising each word with a shake of Brandon's shoulders. This was the first time Brandon had seen this side of his host, and the seriousness in his tone was scary. The little people flew haphazardly around their prison, bumping into surfaces with a muted *dink dink dink,* moths around a light shade. He could hear muted screams of frustration and fury.

"I've heard stories of experienced wood cutters sticking knives through their own eyes because of these little monsters. I get them from a blind woman who lives out in Sussex, believe it or not. The British Countryside is the breeding grounds of the fairy-folk." Horace removed his hands from Brandon's shoulders. "I'll get a plaster for your cut."

"Don't bother," Brandon snapped, "I think I've seen enough. Thanks for the wax worms."

"Woooah. Woooah." Horace held his hands up in a 'hang on a second here' gesture. "You haven't seen the main event yet. The pride and joy of this pet shop."

Pet Shop? Brendan thought. *Now there's a misnomer if ever I've heard one.*

"This cryptid was caught locally, in the forest just beyond

those hills, in fact. Out in the wilds. Have you ever heard of a boggart?"

"No. I mean—maybe?"

"Cryptozoologists tell stories of a creature which haunts the British woodland, waiting in seclusion for an unwary traveller to wander through," Horace said with relish. "The boggart lures the poor sap into the deepest, darkest groves where the sunlight struggles to break through, promising them treasures beyond their wildest dreams. Once trapped, he drains the traveller of all life force, turning them to stone." He pulled out a match and lit his pipe, sending out a fresh blue plume of sweet smoke.

Despite himself, and the dull throb of his forehead, Brandon was intrigued. Five more minutes wouldn't harm anyone, he reasoned. He'd be very careful this time.

"OK Horace, show me, but then I've got to go," he said wiping his forehead with a sleeve. He was relieved to see the bleeding had stopped.

Horace took him through the kitchen. Opening a locked door, He led Brandon up a flight of narrow, wooden steps. "I always said I'd never let anyone see my private quarters, but in your case, I'll make an exception." The old man said. "Just be careful where you step. There's all sorts up here, waiting to go on display."

They walked down a corridor lined on either side with cages. The wild animal scent was unbearable and Brandon pulled up his shirt to cover his nose. He caught glimpses of strange, deformed creatures behind the bars. He guessed from his limited knowledge that one canine-like animal was a chupacabra, and a slimy, green hand reaching to grab his ankle belonged to some sort of goblin. Growls and squawks, screams and howls filled the room. It was like the Bedlam petting zoo.

Horace reached the end of the corridor and turned. He held an ornate key in his leathery hand. "In here," he said, above the noise. He unlocked the door, pushed it open and invited Brandon to enter.

A solitary window illuminated the sparsely decorated

chamber. The only furniture was a neatly made bed. A massive cage, covered by a white sheet, dominated the room. Horace closed the door and approached it eagerly.

"Get a load of this."

He pulled the sheet away with all the aplomb of a stage magician. Inside, stood the statue of a man, bent at the knees, palms raised as if warding something away. His head was turned to the side, eyes closed tightly. A mouth yawned in a silent scream.

Brandon squinted, baffled. "What's that?" he asked. "Where's your boggart?"

The answer dawned on him as Horace removed his flat cap. Two horns protruded from his hairless brow. Brandon ran towards the door, but he knew it would be locked.

"That," Horace told the unwary traveller, his eyes brightening into glowing pools of whirling flame, "used to be the owner of this pet shop."

SEEDED

SUSAN TAITEL

"Do you have any well-known artists?" the woman *[Chose not to be identified - Ed.]* in the vintage Chanel asks, a hint of trepidation in her voice. This is a big decision.

"Of course." Heidi, the proprietress, places a reassuring hand on her shoulder and guides her into the showroom. It's a sleek, nearly empty, space. "How do you feel about Klimt?"

"His paintings are beautiful but a little macabre. All those skulls."

"Perfectly understandable." Heidi clicks her tongue amiably.

"Any other options?"

"Picasso, though not a lot. And Seurat. I shouldn't mention this since there's a waitlist, but Monet could be arranged."

"Monet?" The woman's face brightens, visions of "Water Lilies" dance behind her eyes. Heidi produces a tablet from a drawer. With a few deft swipes, she presents a buyer's guide for Monet.

"I'm afraid that's over my budget." The woman deflates.

"He is sought after." Heidi nods. "What about Toulouse-Lautrec? We have a surplus at the moment."

The woman's brow furrows as she tries to place him. "He did the Can-Can girls?"

"Frequently," Heidi deadpans.

"Wasn't he a midget?"

"He had a bone disorder that stunted his legs, but his talent was immeasurable."

"Still, I don't think..." She glances my way as if seeking my input. All I can recall about Lautrec is that he was dubbed Tripod on account of his impressive 'third leg.' *[Apocryphal - Ed.]*

Heidi can see her sale going astray. "Do you have any interests besides art?" she asks.

"Classical music. You wouldn't have Mozart, would you? I adore Mozart!"

"Our stock doesn't go back that far. But Mahler is available, and Brahms. And we just cleared Tchaikovsky."

"No! Really?"

"Indeed." Heidi nods, her hazel eyes twinkling.

"He's the one. I'll take Tchaikovsky."

"Good choice." Heidi indulges her with a smile. They move to an unobtrusive desk at the back of the showroom.

They review a rundown of the composer's achievements, his medical history, and possible genetic drawbacks. The woman asks few questions. She was sold the moment she heard the name. She signs the contract and eagerly swipes her credit card. Heidi murmurs into an earpiece. Moments later a willowy young woman in a tailored lab coat enters.

She hands over a stylish, brushed copper canister. The woman cradles it to her chest. Though it appears tightly sealed, I wince at its proximity to the vintage silk. Try explaining that to the dry cleaner.

"There's a port on the bottom to test for viability. It's sectioned off from the rest of the specimen. I have a list of labs that can authenticate the DNA. If you return it unthawed in under thirty days, you won't be charged the full amount. But we do keep the deposit."

"Of course. How do I thaw it?"

"When you're ready, push the blue button. It'll be good to go in ten minutes. An applicator is included and there's an instructional video embedded in your e-receipt. We pride ourselves on being user-friendly. If you ask me, it's far less messy than the traditional method." They giggle conspiratorially. Heidi could make a living selling snowmobiles in the Sahara. "There's just one more thing that we ask," she says as the woman pulls on her coat. Prada, if I'm not mistaken.

"Oh, what's that?" The woman pales.

"Send us a picture for the wall!" Heidi beams. With a tap of the tablet, the gleaming wall lights up with several dozen portraits of infants. Each more darling than the last.

"Well." Heidi turns to me once her client has left. "I'm sure your readers have questions."

"Forget the readers, I have questions."

"Come on back." She leads me into a bare white hall and up a flight of stairs.

"I can't let you into the lab. The risk of contamination is too high. But you can look."

She brings me to a glass wall, behind which a passel of technicians work in a room roughly the size of a tennis court. Some take canisters in and out of refrigeration units, while others gaze into microscopes. A few more work at computer stations. Toward the back, a small group sits at an empty table. Each wear a thick visor and black gloves attached to a bundle of wires. Their hands manipulate the air in a manner—let's call it risqué and leave it at that.

Once I've looked my fill, Heidi ushers me into her surprisingly small and cluttered office. Correspondence and spreadsheets litter the desk, while discarded scarves and shoes cover the floor like fallen leaves.

She clears off a chair for me and settles into her own.

"Fire away."

"How does this all work?"

"Generally, the same as your average sperm bank. We've upgraded the basic tech here and there, but our donors are what makes us unique."

"So I've gathered. How do you obtain the samples?"

"I can't go into detail. Our patents haven't been approved yet. But we've developed a method of 'interacting' with donors who are otherwise temporally unavailable."

"If I'm understanding this right, you're using time travel to collect the semen of historical figures?"

"No one is traveling through time." Heidi waves away the notion. "Our technicians are in our time and the donors are in theirs. The only thing making the jump is the specimen."

"You're selling time-traveling sperm."

"Sort of. It does sound a little ridiculous when you put it like that." She chuckles. "But I can't tell you more without revealing proprietary technology."

"Okay, moving on. How do you get the specimen from the donor?"

"I had a feeling we'd be discussing that. Our technology allows for physical interaction, but no communication with the donor. Which is a blessing, actually. Can you imagine the ramifications if they learned about their futures? With this method, there's no chance of altering history."

"But if you can't communicate with them, how do you... get what you need?"

"It's surprisingly simple. You're gonna laugh."

"Try me."

"Nocturnal emission," she says in a stage whisper.

She's right. I do laugh.

"Our technicians are trained to watch for the signs and simply collect the product. And aid the production if necessary."

"Wow." Just wow.

"I know, it took some time for me to get my head around it, and I'm partially responsible for the idea."

"What would you say to those who'd accuse you of stealing from the dead?"

Heidi stiffens. "They aren't dead in the moment. They're only dead now. And is it really stealing if it's something that would otherwise go to waste? We never interfere with product the donor is using."

"But you are taking it without permission."

"We're aware it's a concern. If we could have them sign a waiver, we would. Sometimes a line or two gets crossed in the name of innovation. Which is why we've drawn up a set of ethical guidelines which we take very seriously."

"Such as?"

"First, no war criminals. Hitler's DNA will not be available through our service. Not Pol Pot or Idi Amin either. No one even remotely connected to a genocide.

"Second, the mentally ill are off limits. Not just because of the genetic liabilities, but because we'd never take advantage of someone in that state."

"Then you do consider it taking advantage? But it's okay for the mentally sound?"

"No, no, no, not at all. We just don't want to risk the possibility of exacerbating a delicate condition."

"So, there'll be no little van Goghs in the near future?"

"Never! Finally, we don't use anyone currently living, or with living spouses, siblings, children, or grandchildren."

"Why's that?"

"It would just be weird. You know?"

"I suppose. So, to be clear, I could be impregnated by the historical figure of my choice? Like right now?"

"Yes and no. It has to be a male historical figure. For obvious reasons. And if you wanted it immediately, they'd need to be in our stock. We do special orders if the person fits our parameters. But we need to be certain the sample is up to our standards, which can take weeks of testing. And we can't go further back than 1866."

"Why not?"

"Our machines tend to short around September 21st, 1866. We're looking into it."

"So, I can have JFK's baby, but not Alexander the Great's?"

"Neither, actually. Kennedy still has living grandchildren. I sometimes wish we could waive that rule. We keep getting requests for Chaplin. But he had kids well into his seventies, and then they had kids. And they just live forever!"

"So, as much as I may want to get my hands on Benjamin Franklin's spunk, it's not going to happen?"

"Not with the current technology, but who knows what's down the road? What do you say? Should we schedule a consultation?"

I decline, but I'd be lying if I said I'm not tempted. I'll let others debate the implications of this venture. *[Check later today for editorials from our science, ethics, and economics teams - Ed.]* All I can say, is my biological clock is ticking, and I've always wanted a Klimt.

THE GHOST-EXTINGUISHER
By Gelett Burgess

My attention was first called to the possibility of manufacturing a practicable ghost-extinguisher by a real estate agent in San Francisco.

"There's one thing," he said, "that affects city property here in a curious way. You know we have a good many murders, and, as a consequence, certain houses attain a very sensational and undesirable reputation. These houses are almost impossible to let; you can scarcely get a decent family to occupy them rent-free. Then we have a great many places said to be haunted. These were dead timber on my hands until I happened to notice that the Japanese have no objections to spooks. Now, whenever I have such a building to rent, I let it to a Japanese family at a nominal figure, and after they've taken the curse off, I raise the rent, they move out, the place is renovated, and in the market again."

The subject interested me, for I am not only a scientist, but a speculative philosopher as well. The investigation of those phenomena that lie upon the threshold of the great unknown has always been my favorite field of research. I believed, even then, that the Oriental mind, working along different lines than those which we pursue, has attained knowledge that we know little of.

Thinking, therefore, that these families might have some secret inherited from their misty past, I examined into the matter.

I shall not trouble you with a narration of the incidents which led up to my acquaintance with Hoku Yamanochi. Suffice it to say that I found in him a friend who was willing to share with me his whole lore of quasi-science. I call it this advisedly, for science, as we Occidentals use the term, has to do only with the laws of matter and sensation; our scientific men, in fact, recognize the existence of nothing else. The Buddhistic philosophy, however, goes further.

According to its theories, the soul is sevenfold, consisting of different shells or envelopes—something like an onion—which are shed as life passes from the material to the spiritual state. The first, or lowest, of these is the corporeal body, which, after death, decays and perishes. Next comes the vital principle, which, departing from the body, dissipates itself like an odor, and is lost. Less gross than this is the astral body, which, although immaterial, yet lies near to the consistency of matter. This astral shape, released from the body at death, remains for a while in its earthly environment, still preserving more or less definitely the imprint of the form which it inhabited.

It is this relic of a past material personality, this outworn shell, that appears, when galvanized into an appearance of life, partly materialized, as a ghost. It is not the soul that returns, for the soul, which is immortal, is composed of the four higher spiritual essences that surround the ego, and are carried on into the next life. These astral bodies, therefore, fail to terrify the Buddhists, who know them only as shadows, with no real volition. The Japanese, in point of fact, have learned how to exterminate them.

There is a certain powder, Hoku informed me, which, when burnt in their presence, transforms them from the rarefied, or semi-spiritual, condition to the state of matter. The ghost, so to speak, is precipitated into and becomes a material shape which can easily be disposed of. In this state it is confined and allowed to disintegrate slowly where it can cause no further annoyance.

This long-winded explanation piqued my curiosity, which was not to be satisfied until I had seen the Japanese method applied. It was not long before I had an opportunity. A particularly revolting murder having been committed in San Francisco, my friend Hoku Yamanochi applied for the house, and, after the police had finished their examination, he was permitted to occupy it for a half-year at the ridiculous price of three dollars a month. He invited me to share his quarters, which were large and luxuriously furnished.

For a week, nothing abnormal occurred. Then, one night, I was awakened by terrifying groans followed by a blood-curdling shriek which seemed to emerge from a large closet in my room, the scene of the late atrocity. I confess that I had all the covers pulled over my head and was shivering with horror when my Japanese friend entered, wearing a pair of flowered-silk pajamas. Hearing his voice, I peeped forth, to see him smiling reassuringly.

"You some kind of very foolish fellow," he said. "I show you how to fix him!"

He took from his pocket three conical red pastils, placed them upon a saucer and lighted them. Then, holding the fuming dish in one outstretched hand, he walked to the closed door and opened it. The shrieks burst out afresh, and, as I recalled the appalling details of the scene which had occurred in this very room only five weeks ago, I shuddered at his temerity. But he was quite calm.

Soon, I saw the wraith-like form of the recent victim dart from the closet. She crawled under my bed and ran about the room, endeavoring to escape, but was pursued by Hoku, who waved his smoking plate with indefatigable patience and dexterity.

At last he had her cornered, and the specter was caught behind a curtain of odorous fumes. Slowly the figure grew more distinct, assuming the consistency of a heavy vapor, shrinking somewhat in the operation. Hoku now hurriedly turned to me.

"You hurry up, bring me one pair bellows pretty quick!" he commanded.

I ran into his room and brought the bellows from his fireplace. These he pressed flat, and then carefully inserting one toe of the ghost into the nozzle and opening the handles steadily, he sucked in a portion of the unfortunate woman's anatomy, and dexterously squirted the vapor into a large jar, which had been placed in the room for the purpose. Two more operations were necessary to withdraw the phantom completely from the corner and empty it into the jar. At last the transfer was effected and the receptacle securely stoppered and sealed.

"In formeryore-time," Hoku explained to me, "old priests sucked ghost with mouth and spit him to inside of vase with accuracy. Modern-time method more better for stomach and epiglottis."

"How long will this ghost keep?" I inquired.

"Oh, about four, five hundred years, maybe," was his reply. "Ghost now change from spirit to matter, and comes under legality of matter as usual science."

"What are you going to do with her?" I asked.

"Send him to Buddhist temple in Japan. Old priest use him for high ceremony," was the answer.

My next desire was to obtain some of Hoku Yamanochi's ghost-powder and analyze it. For a while it defied my attempts, but, after many months of patient research, I discovered that it could be produced, in all its essential qualities, by means of a fusion of formaldehyde and hypophenyltrybrompropionic acid in an electrified vacuum. With this product I began a series of interesting experiments.

As it became necessary for me to discover the habitat of ghosts in considerable numbers, I joined the American Society for Psychical Research, thus securing desirable information in regard to haunted houses. These I visited persistently, until my powder was perfected and had been proved efficacious for the capture of any ordinary house-broken phantom. For a while I contented myself with the mere sterilization of these specters, but, as I became surer of success, I began to attempt the transfer of ghosts to receptacles wherein they could be transported and studied at my leisure, classified and preserved for future reference.

Hoku's bellows I soon discarded in favor of a large-sized bicycle-pump, and eventually I had constructed one of my own, of a pattern which enabled me to inhale an entire ghost at a single stroke. With this powerful instrument I was able to compress even an adult life-sized ghost into a two-quart bottle, in the neck of which a sensitive valve (patented) prevented the specter from emerging during process.

My invention was not yet, however, quite satisfactory. While I had no trouble in securing ghosts of recent creation—spirits, that is, who were yet of almost the consistency of matter—on several of my trips abroad in search of material I found in old manor houses or ruined castles many specters so ancient that they had become highly rarefied and tenuous, being at times scarcely visible to the naked eye. Such elusive spirits are able to pass through walls and elude pursuit with ease. It became necessary for me to obtain some instrument by which their capture could be conveniently effected.

The ordinary fire-extinguisher of commerce gave me the hint as to how the problem could be solved. One of these portable hand-instruments I filled with the proper chemicals. When inverted, the ingredients were commingled in vacuo and a vast volume of gas was liberated. This was collected in the reservoir provided with a rubber tube having a nozzle at the end. The whole apparatus being strapped upon my back, I was enabled to direct a stream of powerful precipitating gas in any desired direction, the flow being under control through the agency of a small stopcock. By means of this ghost-extinguisher I was enabled to pursue my experiments as far as I desired.

So far my investigations had been purely scientific, but before long the commercial value of my discovery began to interest me. The ruinous effects of spectral visitations upon real estate induced me to realize some pecuniary reward from my ghost-extinguisher, and I began to advertise my business. By degrees, I became known as an expert in my original line, and my professional services were sought with as much confidence as those of a veterinary surgeon. I manufactured the Gerrish Ghost-Extinguisher in several sizes, and put it on the market, following this venture with the introduction of my justly celebrated Gerrish Ghost-Grenades. These hand-implements were made to be kept in racks conveniently distributed in country houses for cases of sudden emergency. A single grenade, hurled at any spectral form, would, in breaking, liberate enough formaldybrom to coagulate the most perverse spirit, and the resulting vapor could easily be removed from the room by a housemaid with a common broom.

This branch of my business, however, never proved profitable, for the appearance of ghosts, especially in the United States, is seldom anticipated. Had it been possible for me to invent a preventive as well as a remedy, I might now be a millionaire; but there are limits even to modern science.

Having exhausted the field at home, I visited England in the hope of securing customers among the country families there. To my surprise, I discovered that the possession of a family specter was considered as a permanent improvement to the property, and my offers of service in ridding houses of ghostly tenants awakened the liveliest resentment. As a layer of ghosts, I was much lower in the social scale than a layer of carpets.

Disappointed and discouraged, I returned home to make a further study of the opportunities of my invention. I had, it seemed, exhausted the possibilities of the use of unwelcome phantoms. Could I not, I thought, derive a revenue from the traffic in desirable specters? I decided to renew my investigations.

The nebulous spirits preserved in my laboratory, which I had graded and classified, were, you will remember, in a state of suspended animation. They were, virtually, embalmed apparitions, their inevitable decay delayed, rather than prevented. The assorted ghosts that I had now preserved in hermetically sealed tins were thus in a state of unstable equilibrium. The tins once opened and the vapor allowed to dissipate, the original astral body would in time be reconstructed and the warmed-over specter would continue its previous career. But this process, when naturally performed, took years. The interval was quite too long for the phantom to be handled in any commercial way. My problem was, therefore, to produce from my tinned Essence of Ghost a specter that was capable of immediately going into business and that could haunt a house while you wait.

It was not until radium was discovered that I approached the solution of my great problem, and even then months of indefatigable labor were necessary before the process was perfected. It has now been well demonstrated that the emanations of radiant energy sent forth by this surprising element defy our former scientific conceptions of the constitution of matter. It was for me to prove that the vibratory activity of radium (whose amplitudes and intensity are undoubtedly four-dimensional) effects a sort of allotropic modification in the particles of that imponderable ether which seems to lie halfway between matter and pure spirit. This is as far as I need to go in my explanation, for a full discussion involves the use of quaternions and the method of least squares. It will be sufficient for the layman to know that my preserved phantoms, rendered radioactive, would, upon contact with the air, resume their spectral shape.

The possible extension of my business now was enormous, limited only by the difficulty in collecting the necessary stock. It was by this time almost as difficult to get ghosts as it was to get radium. Finding that a part of my stock had spoiled, I was now possessed of only a few dozen cans of apparitions, many of these being of inferior quality. I immediately set about replenishing my raw material. It was not enough for me to pick up a ghost here and there, as one might get old mahogany; I determined to procure my phantoms in wholesale lots.

Accident favored my design. In an old volume of Blackwood's Magazine I happened, one day, to come across an interesting article upon the battle of Waterloo. It mentioned, incidentally, a legend to the effect that every year, upon the anniversary of the celebrated victory, spectral squadrons had been seen by the peasants charging battalions of ghostly grenadiers. Here was my opportunity.

I made elaborate preparations for the capture of this job lot of phantoms upon the next anniversary of the fight. Hard by the fatal ditch which engulfed Napoleon's cavalry I stationed a corps of able assistants provided with rapid-fire extinguishers ready to enfilade the famous sunken road. I stationed myself with a No. 4 model magazine-hose, with a four-inch nozzle, directly in the path which I knew would be taken by the advancing squadron.

It was a fine, clear night, lighted, at first, by a slice of new moon; but later, dark, except for the pale illumination of the stars. I have seen many ghosts in my time—ghosts in garden and garret, at noon, at dusk, at dawn, phantoms fanciful, and specters sad and spectacular—but never have I seen such an impressive sight as this nocturnal charge of cuirassiers, galloping in goblin glory to their time-honored doom. From afar the French reserves presented the appearance of a nebulous mass, like a low-lying cloud or fogbank, faintly luminous, shot with fluorescent gleams. As the squadron drew nearer in its desperate charge, the separate forms of the troopers shaped themselves, and the galloping guardsmen grew ghastly with supernatural splendor.

Although I knew them to be immaterial and without mass or weight, I was terrified at their approach, fearing to be swept under the hoofs of the nightmares they rode. Like one in a dream, I started to run, but in another instant they were upon me, and I

Drawn by George T. Tobin

*"The cut was piled full of frenzied, scrambling specters, as rank after
rank swept down into the horrid gut"*

turned on my stream of formaldybrom. Then I was overwhelmed in a cloud-burst of wild warlike wraiths.

The column swept past me, over the bank, plunging to its historic fate. The cut was piled full of frenzied, scrambling specters, as rank after rank swept down into the horrid gut. At last the ditch swarmed full of writhing forms and the carnage was dire.

My assistants with the extinguishers stood firm, and although almost unnerved by the sight, they summoned their courage, and directed simultaneous streams of formaldybrom into the struggling mass of fantoms. As soon as my mind returned, I busied myself with the huge tanks I had prepared for use as receivers. These were fitted with a mechanism similar to that employed in portable forges, by which the heavy vapor was sucked off. Luckily the night was calm, and I was enabled to fill a dozen cylinders with the precipitated ghosts. The segregation of individual forms was, of course, impossible, so that men and horses were mingled in a horrible mixture of fricasseed spirits. I intended subsequently to empty the soup into a large reservoir and allow the separate specters to reform according to the laws of spiritual cohesion.

Circumstances, however, prevented my ever accomplishing this result. I returned home, to find awaiting me an order so large and important that I had no time in which to operate upon my cylinders of cavalry.

My patron was the proprietor of a new sanatorium for nervous invalids, located near some medicinal springs in the Catskills. His building was unfortunately located, having been built upon the site of a once-famous summer hotel, which, while filled with guests, had burnt to the ground, scores of lives having been lost. Just before the patients were to be installed in the new structure, it was found that the place was haunted by the victims of the conflagration to a degree that rendered it inconvenient as a health resort. My professional services were requested, therefore, to render the building a fitting abode for convalescents. I wrote to the proprietor, fixing my charge at five thousand dollars. As my usual rate was one hundred dollars per ghost, and over a hundred lives were lost at the fire, I considered this price reasonable, and my offer was accepted.

The sanatorium job was finished in a week. I secured one hundred and two superior spectral specimens, and upon my return to the laboratory, put them up in heavily embossed tins with attractive labels in colors.

My delight at the outcome of this business was, however, soon transformed to anger and indignation. The proprietor of the health resort, having found that the specters from his place had been sold, claimed a rebate upon the contract price equal to the value of the modified ghosts transferred to my possession. This, of course, I could not allow. I wrote, demanding immediate payment according to our agreement, and this was peremptorily refused. The manager's letter was insulting in the extreme. The Pied Piper of Hamelin was not worse treated than I felt myself to be; so, like the piper, I determined to have my revenge.

I got out the twelve tanks of Waterloo ghost-hash from the storerooms, and treated them with radium for two days. These I shipped to the Catskills billed as hydrogen gas. Then, accompanied by two trustworthy assistants, I went to the sanatorium and preferred my demand for payment in person. I was ejected with contumely. Before my hasty exit, however, I had the satisfaction of noticing that the building was filled with patients. Languid ladies were seated in wicker chairs upon the piazzas, and frail anemic girls filled the corridors. It was a hospital of nervous wrecks whom the slightest disturbance would throw into a panic. I suppressed all my finer feelings of mercy and kindness and smiled grimly as I walked back to the village.

That night was black and lowering, fitting weather for the pandemonium I was about to turn loose. At ten o'clock, I loaded a wagon with the tanks of compressed cohorts, and, muffled in heavy overcoats, we drove to the sanatorium. All was silent as we

Drawn by George T. Tobin

"I fled, but Napoleon's men fled with me"

approached; all was dark. The wagon concealed in a grove of pines, we took out the tanks one by one, and placed them beneath the ground-floor windows. The sashes were easily forced open, and raised enough to enable us to insert the rubber tubes connected with the iron reservoirs. At midnight everything was ready.

I gave the word, and my assistants ran from tank to tank, opening the stopcocks. With a hiss as of escaping steam the huge vessels emptied themselves, vomiting forth clouds of vapor, which, upon contact with the air, coagulated into strange shapes as the white of an egg does when dropped into boiling water. The rooms became instantly filled with dismembered shades of men and horses seeking wildly to unite themselves with their proper parts.

Legs ran down the corridors, seeking their respective trunks, arms writhed wildly reaching for missing bodies, heads rolled hither and yon in search of native necks. Horses' tails and hoofs whisked and hurried in quest of equine ownership until, reorganized, the spectral steeds galloped about to find their riders.

Had it been possible, I would have stopped this riot of wraiths long ere this, for it was more awful than I had anticipated, but it was already too late. Cowering in the garden, I began to hear the screams of awakened and distracted patients. In another moment, the front door of the hotel was burst open, and a mob of hysterical women in expensive nightgowns rushed out upon the lawn, and huddled in shrieking groups.

I fled into the night.

I fled, but Napoleon's men fled with me. Compelled by I know not what fatal astral attraction, perhaps the subtle affinity of the creature for the creator, the spectral shells, moved by some mysterious mechanics of spiritual being, pursued me with fatuous fury. I sought refuge, first, in my laboratory, but, even as I approached, a lurid glare foretold me of its destruction. As I drew nearer, the whole ghost-factory was seen to be in flames; every moment crackling reports were heard, as the overheated tins of phantasmagoria exploded and threw their supernatural contents upon the night. These liberated ghosts joined the army of Napoleon's outraged warriors, and turned upon me. There was not enough formaldybrom in all the world to quench their fierce energy. There was no place in all the world safe for me from their visitation. No ghost-extinguisher was powerful enough to lay the host of spirits that haunted me henceforth, and I had neither time nor money left with which to construct new Gatling quick-firing tanks.

It is little comfort to me to know that one hundred nervous invalids were completely restored to health by means of the terrific shock which I administered.

Author Interview
Kelly A. Harmon
with Andrew McCurdy

Kelly, I just wanted to start off by thanking you for agreeing to do this interview. To begin, I was struck at once by the opening sentence for On the Path, it sets the tone beautifully for what follows. What was the genesis of the idea behind this story?

Kelly: Thank you! Beginnings are so hard. I toyed with that one for a long time, and finally decided to just get to the point.

This story started with me noodling over the idea of alternate fuel sources. I'd worked my way through the obvious, and finally stumbled over "souls." Then the questions started: How does one obtain souls to run the engine? How old are the souls? Were the souls willing to labor for anyone? What if a soul wanted to escape? I built the story around the answers to these questions. (Which is so upside-down from my usual process! My prevailing routine is to start with an interesting character, put them in a terrible situation, and see where the story goes from there...)

What role does research play in your writing?

Kelly: Most of my research is fact-checking. I write an urban fantasy series—Charm City Darkness—about a woman who tries to help someone out and winds up demon-marked. I mention real street names and describe exorcisms and other church rites. And even though I was raised Catholic—in Baltimore, where the series takes place—I am constantly checking my facts about the city and the church. No matter how well I think I remember details, there's always something I've forgotten.

To a lesser extent, I use research for story ideas, but it's usually serendipity. A few years ago I saw a painting by Peter Blume called Nature and Metamorphosis which included Blume's rendition of Tasso's Oak. Research on the Italian poet Torquato Tasso—who supposedly planted this oak—led me tangentially to Pope Clement VIII. Clement is said to have "blessed" coffee so the Catholics could drink it, because it was so tasty, it would be a shame to leave it to the Muslims. Out of that came my story, "The Devil's Brew."

You have a number of published works to your credit. What is your writing process? For example, do you set personal goals, such as daily word counts, number of hours, or specific times of the day to write?

Kelly: It's my nature to always be open to a story. Everything I see, every conversation I hear, everything I *feel* is fodder. I carry a notebook and jot down observations. But it's rare I'll stop there. If I note something of interest, my mind is usually plowing ahead with the story, so I'll write some of that, too. It's a bit of a curse actually—lots and lots of pieces in the boneyard. Eventually, though, I cobble them together.

From a more practical standpoint, I set goals and numbers. Among my fiction goals for 2018, is another Charm City Darkness novel and several short stories. I've broken down the word-count estimates into daily "must do" requirements and I work on them in the evening—once I'm home from the day job. If I hit those targets, I've got some other projects I'd like to complete this year.

As a follow-up, what is your process for editing your work once you have finished a draft?

Kelly: I rarely get to the end of anything before I start to tinker with it.   I like to get a few thousand words down on paper and then go back and expand. As I write, I cycle back through the work I've already written, smoothing, tinkering, cutting and expanding. Once I finally get to the end, I've usually got a fairly solid draft. I then send it to my writer friends—we meet monthly for a meal and critiques—and they provide suggestions.   I take one more pass at it based on their feedback, then I'm done.

How often do you read for pleasure, and what do you look for when you read the works of other authors? Conversely, what are some of your pet peeves about works you have not enjoyed?

Kelly: I read every night before bed—which is probably the worst time for me to indulge. I have a hard time putting down the book and turning off the light!

I read all kinds of books: histories, biographies, any kind of fiction, though I'm partial to fantasy when I'm looking to relax. I want strong characters that captivate and lean prose which keeps me turning pages. I love a well-crafted story with high highs and low lows which, together, make me feel like I've been through the wringer. I want to be exhausted when I close the book for the last time.

I'm pretty forgiving when it comes to writing, especially if the story is interesting. But, I don't like stories with idiot characters. This is the kind of plot that would completely fall apart if the characters had only said or done the obvious in their particular situation. The drama often feels false, the story contrived. As soon as the plot feels forced, I move on to the next book.

What do value the most in feedback and reviews from your readers?

Kelly: I adore readers who take the time to leave *any* feedback! I especially love it when they write about their favorite scenes or favorite character. (It tickles me when their favorite character is also mine!)

Finally, what do you enjoy most about being a writer?

Kelly: The question sounds so simple. The answer does, too: I enjoy telling stories. But it's so much more than that, because I can't remember a time when I was *not* telling stories—to my parents, to my friends, to myself. For me, it's like being possessed —or catching a fever: it's not something I chose. Instead, *writing chose me.* I couldn't stop if I wanted to. (I know, I've tried!)

But I do love a blank white page! And then I love letting the words fall out of my fingertips, filling the page with text. Writing is conjuring something out of nothing. Writing is magic.

CONTRIBUTORS

Gavin Bradley is an Irish writer from Belfast who works in happy obscurity in Edmonton, Alberta. His poetry has recently been selected for the Hennessy New Irish Writing award and his work can be found in *Glass Buffalo, The Open Ear,* and *The Caterpillar* literary magazines, as well as various fantastical anthologies, such as *Frozen Fairy Tales, Ignis Fatuus, Weird Tales: Dark Lane Vol. 3,* and the upcoming *Tesseracts 21.*

Gary Buller is an author from Manchester, England where he lives with his partner Lisa, and daughters Holly and Evie. Raised in the Peak District, hauntingly beautiful landscapes inspired him to write. He is a huge fan of all things macabre, and loves a tale with a twist. Gary is an associate member of the Horror Writers Association. Follow him online @garybuller and garybuller.com.

Gelett Burgess (1866-1951) earned a degree from MIT then escaped west and became part of the San Francisco Bay Area literary renaissance of the 1890s as an artist, poet, author, and humorist. He was best known as a writer of nonsense verse, such as "The Purple Cow," and for introducing French modern art to the United States in an essay titled The "Wild Men of Paris." He was also the author of the *Goops*, a series of illustrated manner books for children, and coined the term *blurb.*

Eric Cline is a writer living in Maryland with his wife and Greyhound (a dog, not a motorized vehicle). He has a Masters degree in English. His works have appeared in *Ellery Queen Mystery Magazine, Galaxy's Edge* (edited by Mike Resnick), *Alfred Hitchcock Mystery Magazine,* the *Writers of the Future* anthology (volume 29) and other places. His story "Elizabethtown" was nominated for the Sidewise Award for Alternate History (Short Form) in 2015.

Laura Duerr is a writer and social media coordinator from Vancouver, Washington, where she lives with her husband, their rescue dog, and too many cats. She is a lifelong Pacific Northwest resident and has a BA in Creative Writing from Linfield College. Her other stories have appeared in *Escape Pod, Shoreline of Infinity,* and *Mad Scientist Journal.*

Kevin Frost is a social hermit sailing the vast sagebrush seas of northern New Mexico. He can often be found managing the Curiosities inbox while eating green chili cheeseburgers at a lonely crossroads diner. When the weather is fine, he works on his house.

Kelly A. Harmon used to write truthful, honest stories about authors and thespians, senators and statesmen, movie stars and murderers. Now she writes lies, which is infinitely more satisfying, but lacks the convenience of doorstep delivery. She is an award-winning journalist and author, and a member of Science Fiction & Fantasy Writers of America. A Baltimore native, she writes the *Charm City Darkness* series. Book 4, *In the Eye of the Beholder,* is out now.

Andrew McCurdy is a writer and editor whose day job as a Speech-Language Pathologist involves helping nonverbal, special needs children access technology to maximize their ability to communicate. He lives in rural Nova Scotia with a ten-year-old girl and two cats. He credits Charleton Heston's angst while kneeling in the surf, cursing the half-buried Statue of Liberty, as the genesis for his love of science fiction.

Julia K. Patt is a writer, teacher, and editor living in Maryland. Her stories have appeared in *Clarkesworld, Escape Pod,* and *Luna Station Quarterly,* among other places. Follow her on Twitter @chidorme or check out her website juliakpatt.com for more.

Holly Schofield travels through time at the rate of one second per second, oscillating between the alternate realities of city and country life. Her stories have appeared in *Analog, Lightspeed, Escape Pod,* and many others publications throughout the world. Find her at hollyschofield.wordpress.com.

Ann Stolinsky is the founder and owner of Gontza Games, an independent board and card game company. Her website is www.gontzagames.com. She is also a partner in Gemini Wordsmiths, a full-service copyediting and content creating company. Visit geminiwordsmiths.com for more information and testimonials. Several of her stories have been published in the last few years.

Susan Taitel grew up in Chicago. She now lives in Minnesota. She has not yet resigned herself to the winters but has been known to say "oh yeah, you betcha" unironically. Susan is a Viable Paradise graduate and has been published by *McSweeneys.net.* She blogs at the imaginatively named susantaitel.com.

Justin Tiang is a Singapore-based concept artist and illustrator for games, television, and film. Justin is pledged to Wonder, which he is able to find just about everywhere. He sings, wanders, and rears bugs for hobbies. View more of his work at tiangpong.com and 28crucis.deviantart.com

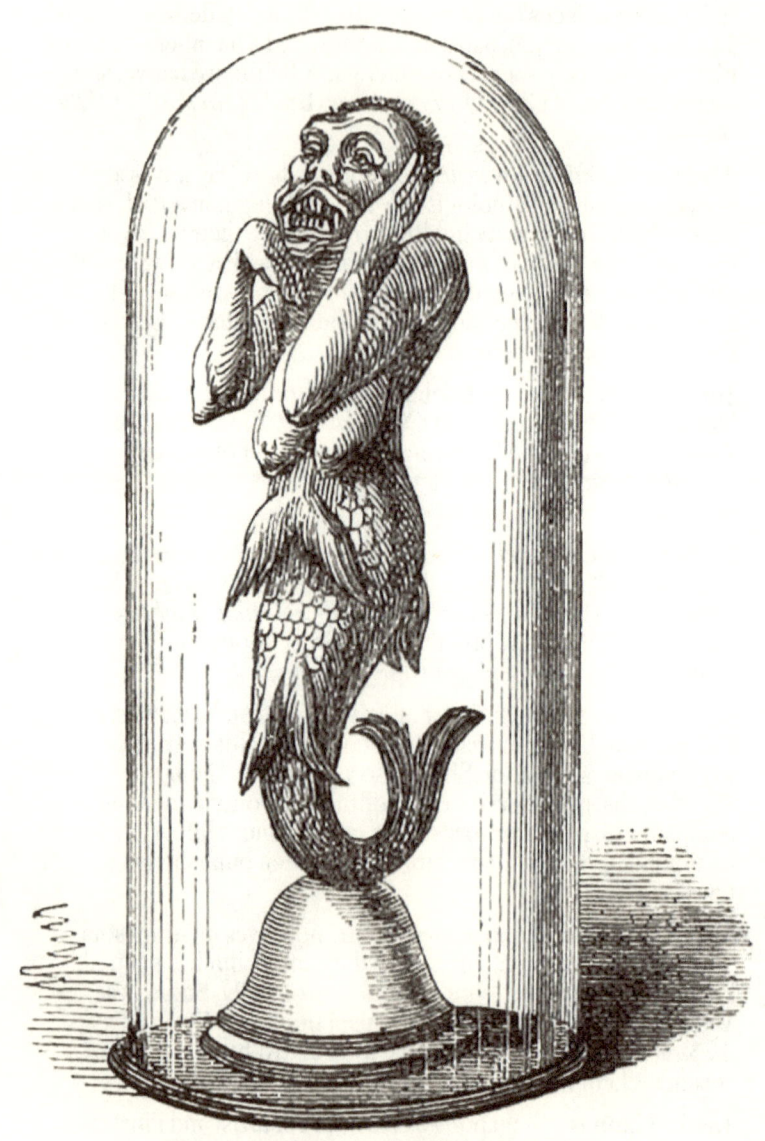

THE MERMAID.

www.ingramcontent.com/pod-product-compliance
Lightning Source LLC
Chambersburg PA
CBHW030633130626
46552CB00002B/824